William Allen White

The Real Issue

William Allen White

The Real Issue

ISBN/EAN: 9783337000929

Printed in Europe, USA, Canada, Australia, Japan

Cover: Foto ©Andreas Hilbeck / pixelio.de

More available books at **www.hansebooks.com**

THE REAL ISSUE

THE REAL ISSUE

BY
WILLIAM ALLEN WHITE

CHICAGO
WAY AND WILLIAMS
1896

CONTENTS

THE REAL ISSUE

The Real Issue

IT was near the close of a long session—
a session which had lasted a winter and
a spring and a summer, and threatened to
push itself into the first days of autumn,
when Wharton, the Western member, who
had been in the house five terms, concluded
to pack his valise and go home. The campaign was growing warm. Nearly all of the
county conventions had been held, and a
majority of the delegates elected were in-
structed for him, which insured his renomination if the three remaining counties in
the district did not go solidly against him.
He had laid his plans mechanically for a
renomination, and if he had stopped to ask
himself whether or not he really wanted to
come back to congress, he would probably
have said no. He was tired, but he did
not know why. He thought he needed

rest, that he had been overworked, that he was played out; yet his private secretary, who kept the run of the pension business and did his routine work, did not seem tired,—the private secretary even had refused a vacation, and it was at the secretary's own request that he stayed in Washington.

But Wharton, the Western member, was tired,—dead tired; and he pictured to himself the pleasures of going back to his home in the little town of Baxter, where people on the streets who had seen him grow up from a boy and called him "Tom," really were glad to see him. Just before he had left his rooms for the departing train his private secretary had handed him the day's clippings; and after he had been riding for an hour or so, while he was fumbling in his pockets for a match, they tumbled out in a tight little roll. He idly read them. He was used to unjust abuse and sick of uncalled-for praise. The first clipping was taken from the Queen City *Daily Herald;* it bore a Washington date-line, and was introduced

by the words, "Special to the *Herald.*"
It read:

They say here that Wharton of the Fourth
District, is beginning to feel uneasy. He has
received several letters from his district that
have convinced him that the Populist cyclone
has shaken down several lengths of fence in
Lee, Meade and Smith counties. Bill Heat-
ley's strength is said to be developing down
there wonderfully. The Hon. Ike Russell,
who was here last week looking for a job as
receiver of the Baxter National bank, was in
close consultation with Wharton three of the
four nights he was here, and the "old man"
is wearing a hunted look and is talking to
himself. They say down in the Fourth district that it will take more than "Our Tom"
Wharton's hug to explain away his silver vote.

Wharton knew the correspondent and
only smiled as he flipped the wadded clipping out of the car window. There was a
short editorial clipping from the same paper.
It said:

The dispatches say that "Our Tom" Wharton is wiggling in his seat and trying to
project his astral body in the Fourth district
to see how his fences are, and at the same time
to keep his corporeal body in Washington to
look after Ike Russell's pie plate. If "Our

Tom'' doesn't fall down in his anxiety to keep one foot in the "bloody Fourth" and the other at the political bake shop, he must be either a Colossus of Rhodes or a "quadrille dancer.''

Wharton dropped that on the floor and read another from the Smith County *Farmer's Friend*. It was long and full of double leads and "break lines" and italics and exclamation points. It was abusive in the extreme and closed with this tirade:

Now, let us reason together. Tom Wharton has been in Congress ten years; he had been judge six years before entering Congress, and county superintendent four years before he was judge. Twenty years has this man been in office; his total salary in that time has been only $70,000. Yet he is rated by the commercial agencies at one-half million dollars. He has banks and railroad stocks; he owns mortgages and farms. Where did he get them? His time has been sold to the people; he has been false to every trust; he has voted with the East on the money question; he has neglected the farmers at every turn. He is a garden-seed congressman; he comes out here and haw-haws around, and then goes back to vote with Wall street. Wall street knows its friends, and "Our Tom" is worth one-half million dollars, lives in a mansion filled with hammered brass at Baxter, while the farmer foots the bills.

Wharton knew that the editor of the *Farmer's Friend* had been a candidate for the postoffice at Smith City; that he himself had lent the editor money and held his note for $500. He put the clipping in his pocket-book with a sigh, and looked through the other scraps of paper. There were perhaps a dozen—a few of them laudatory to an offensive degree, some clearly bids for money, and the rest a fair discussion of his candidacy.

Wharton's first week in the district was spent at Baxter. He did practically nothing to secure his renomination, although wise-looking men from each of the three doubtful counties came nearly every day to Baxter and went directly from the train to Wharton's house. They all wanted money or promises of "assistance"; and each of them told how some precinct could be "swung into line" by a little work on the part of the certain third person—always nameless,—who would need money for cigars and livery hire.   Wharton put these statesmen off, and they went away doubting whether they would support the "old man" or fight him.   The congressman's presence in the little town was an event, and he had callers all day long who seemed to need help in different ways.   Soldiers desired pensions;   mothers asked for positions in Washington for their sons;   young women called to see about clerkships;   widows, whose husbands he had known, came to borrow money.   He was honestly glad to see all these people and, when he could, he helped them;   he rarely made an enemy, even though he always was frank.

It was Saturday evening, and Wharton was just entering on his second week at home, and he and his friend, "Ike" Russell, were sitting on the southern porch of the congressman's home.   Their wives and daughters were in the parlor around the piano, and the two men were at that preliminary stage of conversation in which ideas are conveyed by grunts and monosyllables.

"What did Hughey of Smith City want to-day?" asked Russell.

"About two hundred, more or less," said the congressman.

"Hughey's a thief; he'd spend about $25, and the rest would go into his jeans."

"I suppose so," Wharton answered. "Say we lose Smith county?"

"Well, you say," said his friend. "Did you see Higgins, from Lee Valley? He told me last month that he had five fellows who could swing Lee county for $100 a piece."

"Ugh," grunted the congressman. "That makes $2,300 so far, if I come down."

"Well, that's cheaper than you got off before—by several hundred."

Wharton yawned, and the silence that followed was broken only by the tinkle of the cow bells in the valley below the town, and the splash of water over the dam across the river that runs around the village. Occasionally the sound of voices singing on the water or the notes of a guitar would come up on the gusts of wind. The piano in the parlor was silent, and the moon was barely visible under the eastern corner of the porch. The men had smoked in silence a few moments when Wharton said:

"Ike, what is the real issue in this campaign?"

"I dunno, old man; sometimes I think it's the tariff; sometimes I think it's silver; and then at other times I just give it all up. What's your idea, Tom?"

The congressman did not reply at once; he seemed to be pulling his ideas together for a longer speech than usual. He twisted his gray moustache nervously; he looked askance at his friend, who was apparently listening to the music that had just started up again in the parlor. Wharton went over to the garden hose which was turned upon a shrub, changed its course, came back, relighting his cigar, and said:

"B'Godfrey, I don't know, Ike, I don't know. Do you remember when we used to cut corn at six cents a shock, and go to school down the valley where those cow bells were tinkling a little while ago? We used to sit on the fence of nights like this and talk 'way into the night about what we were going to do.''

"Yes?" said the politician, expectantly.

"Yes, and I used to hope to go to congress some day; we used to talk of the old-time statesmen and read their speeches in the school readers,—Clay and Calhoun and the great men whose names we knew as boys. They were tall, thin, spare men in swallow-tailed coats and chokers, and hair that looked fierce and statesmanlike. Do you remember the congressman from this district forty years ago; how dignified he was, what a really great man he must have been? He lived greatness every hour of his life. The men who went to the territorial legislature,—how superior they seemed, with their tall hats and close buttoned coats! Ike, do you remember when I went to the legislature in the winter of '70, and came back discouraged and disappointed with the sham of it all — the row and the rings and the schemes?''

Russell would have interjected some reminiscent joke on the young statesman, but Wharton went on as if to keep the thread of the conversation in his teeth.

"Yes, yes, Ike, I know about my plug hat and all that; and then do you remember how I ran for judge and was nominated for congress back in '84 as a dark horse on the three hundreth ballot, and how I was elected and told the people from the box down by the bonfire in the public square that I was going to be worthy of the honor? Ike, the tears I shed there were honest tears, for God knows how proud I was. All these ten years were before me, and what a great ten years I hoped they would be. I thought of my plans as a boy—you and me on the fence down in the valley, Ike—and I looked over all the names in congress then —ten years ago I mean—and they seemed great names to me. I could hardly wait to get to Washington to see the men and to be one of them. I was such a boy, Ike— ten years ago."

Each man puffed his cigar in a moment's pause. Wharton lighted a fresh one. Russell thought in so many words: "It's one of Tom's talkative nights."

Wharton took up the thread where it had dropped.

"Here I am, Ike, a flesh-and-blood statesman. I've been in it and through it. I've held as high a place in the organization of the House as any of the great men we used to read about. I've passed a pension bill — and the old soldiers, for whom I worked night and day during six months, have passed resolutions against me. I have had my name on a silver bill for which the fiat money fellows have abused me. I've led my party through two successful fights. And what is there in it? You know, as well as I do, that it is hollow,—all a hollow show. What's the use of it? Why should a man wear his life out up there in that city just to keep his name in print? There was a man named Keifer—an Ohio man—who was speaker of the house once. Who that reads the papers knows anything of him to-day? Yet he worked his life nearly out to be a statesman. Where are the seconds in the Blaine-Conkling fight? Ike, there's nothing in it. I know, Ike, there's nothing in it but ashes."

The politician said nothing; he did not know how the talk was turning.

"Ike," resumed the congressman, taking a firmer hold on his cigar, and tightly grasping the arms of the chair, "Ike, what's the use? Here comes a lot of Bills and Dicks and Toms and Harrys, who want me to put up $2,300 and promises that I'll be two years working to keep, just to go back there. I go back there and work and fret and stew for this, that and the other thing that I don't care a cent for. I have no heart in it; I feel like a sneak; I have to swallow my pride; I've no ideals; there is no reward; nothing but higgling with a lot of mercenary, impecunious thieves here at home, and log-rolling with a lot of shrewder shysters of the same sort in congress at Washington. If I go on, I must buy my way in; buy my own slavery, Ike, slavery to the fellows I despise. I know I've done it three or four times, but I kept thinking the end would some day justify the means. But it doesn't; it never will; it's a fraud, Ike, and I'm done. I am going to be honest just for once in my life. I don't have to go to congress; I can be lots happier here—here with friends and my family and —now don't laugh old man—and—and— my honor. That's a little stagey, Ike, but that's the real issue in this campaign and I'm out of this fight. Let's go in and hear the music, Ike. That's the end of it, I've thought it all over and I've decided."

Probably most men—at least most moralizing men—would have called the "old man" weak had they seen him the following Monday making out a check payable to Isaac Russell for $2,300. But most men do not know what it is to worship an idol for a lifetime, and they cannot understand how a man can love his idol even when he knows to his bitter sorrow that it is only clay.

The Story of Aqua Pura

PEOPLE who write about Kansas, as a rule, write ignorantly, and speak of the state as a finished product. Kansas, like Gaul of old, is divided into three parts, differing as widely, each from the other, as any three countries in the same latitude upon the globe. It would be as untrue to classify together the Egyptian, the Indian and the Central American, as to speak of the Kansas man without distinguishing between the Eastern Kansan, the Central Kansan, and the Western Kansan. Eastern Kansas is a finished community like New York or Pennsylvania. Central Kansas is finished, but not quite paid for; and Western Kansas, the only place where there is any suffering from drouth or crop failures, is a new country—old only in a pluck which is slowly conquering the desert.

Aqua Pura was a western Kansas town,
set high up, far out on the prairie.   It was
founded nine years ago, at the beginning of
the boom, not by cow-boys and ruffians,
but by honest, ambitious men and women.
Of the six men who staked out the town
site, two — Johnson and Barringer — were
Harvard men; one, Nickols, was from
Princeton; and the other three, Bemis,
Bradley and Hicks, had come from inland
state universities.   When their wives came
west there was a Vassar reunion, and the
first mail that arrived after the postoffice
had been established brought the New
York magazines.   The town was like doz-
ens of others that sprang up far out in the
treacherous wilderness in that fresh, green
spring of 1886.

They called it Aqua Pura, choosing a
Latin name to proclaim to the world that it
was not a rowdy town.   The new yellow
pine of the little village gleamed in the clear
sunlight.   It could be seen for miles on a
clear, warm day, as it stood upon a rise
of ground; and over in Maize, six miles

away, the electric lights of Aqua Pura,
which flashed out in the evening before
the town was six months old, could be
seen distinctly. A school house that cost
twenty thousand dollars was built before
the town had seen its first winter; and
the first Christmas ball in Aqua Pura was
held in an opera house that cost ten thousand. Money was plentiful; two and three
story buildings rose on each side of the
main street of the little place. The farmers who had taken homesteads in the
country around the town had prospered.
The sod had yielded handsomely from the
first breaking. Those who had come too
late to put in crops found it easy to borrow
money. There was an epidemic of hope in
the air. Everyone breathed the contagion.
The public library association raised a thousand dollars for books during the winter,
and in the spring a syndicate was formed to
erect a library building. Aqua Pura could
not afford to be behind other towns, and
the railroad train that passed the place
threw off packages of the newest books as

fast as mails could come from New York. The sheet-iron tower of the Aqua Pura waterworks rose early in the spring of '87, and far out in the high grass the hydrants were scattered. Living water came bountifully from the wells that were sunk from fifty to one hundred feet in the ground.

Barringer was elected mayor at the municipal election in the spring of '87, and he platted out Barringer's Addition, and built a house there with borrowed money in June. There were two thousand people in Aqua Pura then. Hacks rolled prosperously over the smooth, hard, prairie streets; two banks opened; and the newspaper, which was printed the day the town was laid off, became a daily. Society grew gay, and people from all corners of the globe met in the booming village.

There was no lawless element. There was not a saloon in the town. A billiard hall, and a dark room, wherein cards might be played surreptitiously, were the only institutions which made the people of Aqua Pura blush, when they took the innumerable "eastern capitalists" over the town who visited Western Kansas that year. These "capitalists" were entertained at a three-story brick hotel, equipped with electricity and modern plumbing in order to excel Maize, where the hotel was an indifferent frame affair. There were throngs of well-dressed people on the streets, and sleek fat horses were hitched in front of the stores wherein the farmers traded.

This is the story of the rise. Barringer has told it a thousand times. Barringer believed in the town to the last. When the terrible drouth of 1887, with its furnace-like breath singed the town and the farms in Fountain county, Barringer lead the majority which proudly claimed that the country was all right; and as chairman of the board of county commissioners, he sent a scathing message to the Governor, refusing aid. Barringer's own bank loaned money on land, whereon the crop had failed, to tide the farmers over the winter. Barringer's signature guaranteed loans from the east upon everything negotiable, and Aqua Pura thrived for a time upon promises. Here and there, in the spring of 1888, there was an empty building. One room of the opera house block was vacant. Barringer started a man in business, selling notions, who occupied the room. Barringer went east and pleaded with the men who had invested in the town to be easy on their debtors. Then came the hot winds of July, blowing out of the southwest, scorching the grass, shrivelling the grain, and drying up the streams that had filled in the spring. During the fall of that year the hotel, which had been open only in the lower story, closed. The opera house began to be used for "aid" meetings, and when the winter wind blew dust-blackened snow through the desolate streets of the little town, it rattled a hundred windows in vacant houses, and sometimes blew sun-warped boards from the high sidewalk that led across the gully to the big red grade of the unfinished "Chicago Air Line."

Barringer did not go east that year. He could not. But he wrote—wrote regularly

and bravely to the eastern capitalists who
were concerned in his bank and loan company; and they grew colder and colder as
the winter deepened and the interest on
defaulted loans came not. Barringer's fail-
ure was announced in the spring of '89.
Nickols had left. Johnson had left. The
other founders of Aqua Pura had died in
'87-'88, and their families had gone, and
with them went the culture and the ambition of the town. But Barringer held on
and lived, rent free, in the two front rooms
of the barn of a hotel. His daughter,
Mary, frail, tanned, hollow-eyed, and withered by the drouths, lived with him.

In 1890 the hot winds came again in the
summer, and long and steadily they blew,
blighting everything. There were only five
hundred people in Fountain county that
year, and they lived on the taxes from the
railroad that crossed the county. Families
were put on the poor list without disgrace
—it was almost a mark of political distinction—and in the little town many devices

were in vogue to distribute the county funds during the winter.

There was no rain that winter and the snow was hard and dry. Cattle on the range suffered for water and died by the thousands. A procession from the little town started eastward early in the spring. White-canopied wagons, and wagons covered with oil table-cloths of various hues, or clad in patch-work quilts, sought the rising sun.

Barringer grew thin, unkempt and gray. Every evening, when the wind rattled in the deserted rooms of the old hotel, and made the faded signs up and down the dreary street creak, the old man and his daughter went over their books, balancing, accounting interest, figuring on mythical problems that the world had long since forgotten.

Christmas eve, 1891, the entire village, fifteen souls in all, assembled at Barringer's house. He was hopeful, even cheerful, and talked blithely of what "one good crop" would do for the country; although there were no farmers left to plant it, even if nature had beeen harboring a smile for the dreary land. The year that followed that Christmas promised much. There were spring rains, and in May, the brown grass and the scattered patches of wheat grew green and fair to see. Barringer freshened up perceptibly. He sent an account of his indebtedness—on home-ruled manilla paper —to his creditors in the east, and faithfully assured them that he would remit all he owed in the fall. A few wanderers straggled into Fountain county, lured by the green fields and running brooks. The gray prairie wolf gave up the dug-out to human occupants. Lights in the prairie cabins twinkled back hope to the stars. Before June there were a thousand people in Fountain county. Aqua Pura's business-houses seemed to liven up. There was a Fourth-of-July celebration in town. But the rain that spoiled the advertised "fire-works in the evening" was the last that fell until winter. A car load of aid from Central Kansas saved a hundred lives in Fountain county that year.

When the spring of 1893 opened, Barringer looked ten years older than he looked the spring before. The grass on the range was sere, and great cracks were in the earth. The winter had been dry. The spring opened dry, with high winds blowing through May. There were but five people on the townsite that summer, Barringer, his daughter, and the postmaster's family. Supplies came overland from Maize. A bloody county-seat war had given the rival town the prize in 1890. Barringer had plenty of money to buy food, for the county commissioners distributed the taxes which the railroad paid.

It was his habit to sit on the front porch of the deserted hotel and look across the prairies to the southwest and watch the breaking clouds scatter into the blue of the twilight. He could see the empty water tower silhouetted against the sky. The frame buildings that rose in the boom days had all been moved away, the line of the horizon was guarded at regular intervals by the iron hydrants far out on the prairie, that stood like sentinels hemming in the past. The dying wind seethed through the short, brown grass. Heat lightning winked devilishly in the distance, and the dissolving clouds that gathered every afternoon laughed in derisive thunder at the hopes of the worn old man sitting on the warped boards of the hotel porch. Night after night he sat there, waiting, with his daughter by his side. There had been a time when he was too proud to go to the east, where his name was a by-word. Now he was too poor in purse and in spirit. So he sat and waited, hoping fondly for the realization of a dream which he feared could never come true.

There were days when the postmaster's four-year-old child sat with him. The old man and the child sat thus one evening when the old man sighed: "If it would only rain, there would be half a crop yet! If it would only rain!" The child heard him and sighed imitatively: "Yes, if it would only rain—what is rain, Mr. Barringer?" He looked at the child blankly and sat for a

long time in silence. When he arose he
did not even have a pretence of hope. He
grew despondent from that hour, and a sort
of hypochondria seized him. It was his
fancy to exaggerate the phenomena of the
drouth.

That fall when the winds piled the sand
in the railroad "cuts" and the prairie was
as hard and barren as the ground around a
cabin door, Barringer's daughter died of
fever. The old man seemed little moved
by sorrow. But as he rode back from the
bleak grave-yard, through the sand cloud,
in the carriage with the dry, rattling spokes,
he could only mutter to the sympathizing
friends who had come from Maize to
mourn with him, "And we laid her in the
hot and dusty tomb." He recalled an old
song which fitted these words, and for days
kept crooning: "Oh, we laid her in the hot
and dusty tomb."

That winter the postmaster left. The
office was discontinued. The county commissioners tried to get Barringer to leave.
He would not be persuaded to go. The

county commissioners were not insistent.
It gave one of them an excuse for drawing
four dollars a day from the county treasury;
he rode from Maize to Aqua Pura every day
with supplies for Barringer.

The old man cooked, ate, and slept in the
office of the hotel. Day after day he put
on his overcoat in the winter and made the
rounds of the vacant store buildings. He
walked up and down in the little paths
through the brown weeds in the deserted
streets, all day long, talking to himself.
At night, when the prairie wind rattled
through the empty building, blowing snow
and sand down the halls, and in little drifts
upon the broken stairs, the old man's lamp
was seen by straggling travellers burning far
into the night. He told his daily visitor
that he was keeping his books.

Thus the winter passed. The grass came
with the light mists of March. By May
it had lost its color. By June it was brown,
and the hot winds came again in August,
curving the warped boards a little deeper
on the floor of the hotel porch. Herders

and travellers, straggling back to the green
country, saw him sitting there at twilight,
looking toward the southwest,—a grizzled,
unkempt old man, with a shifting light in
his eye. To such as spoke to him he always
made the same speech: "Yes, it looks like
rain, but it can't rain. The rain has gone
dry out here. They say it rained at
Hutchinson,—maybe so, I doubt it. There
is no God west of Newton. He dried up in
'90. They talk irrigation. That's an old
story in hell. Where's Johnson? Not here!
Where's Nickols? Not here! Bemis? Not
here! Bradley? Not here! Hicks? Not
here! Where's handsome Dick Barringer,
Hon. Richard Barringer? Here! Here he is,
holding down a hot brick in a cooling room of
hell! Yes, it does look like rain, does n't
it?"

Then he would go over it all again, and
finally cross the trembling threshold of the
hotel, slamming the crooked, sun-steamed
door behind him. There he stayed, summer and winter, looking out across the
burned horizon, peering at the long, low,

black line of clouds in the southwest, longing for the never-coming rain.

Cattle roamed the streets in the early
spring, but the stumbling of the animals
upon the broken walks, did not disturb him,
and the winds and the drouth soon drove
them away. The messenger with provisions
came every morning. The summer, with
its awful heat, began to glow. The lightning and the thunder joked insolently in
the distance at noon; and the stars in the
deep, dry blue looked down and mocked
the old man's prayers as he sat, at night,
on his rickety sentry box. He tottered
through the deserted stores calling his roll.
Night after night he walked to the red clay
grade of the uncompleted "Air Line" and
looked over the dead level stretches of
prairie. He would have gone away, but
something held him to the town. Here
he had risked all. Here, perhaps, in his
warped fancy, he hoped to regain all. He
had written so often, " Times will be
better in the spring," that it was part of his
confession of faith—that and "One good

crop will bring the country around all right." This was written with red clay in the old man's nervous hand on the side of the hotel, on the faded signs, on the deserted inner walls of the stores,—in fact, everywhere in Aqua Pura.

The wind told on him; it withered him, sapped his energy, and hobbled his feet.

One morning he awoke and a strange sound greeted his ears. There was a gentle tapping in the building and a roar that was not the guffaw of the wind. He rushed for the door. He saw the rain, and bareheaded he ran to the middle of the streets where it was pouring down. The messenger from Maize with the day's supplies found him standing there, vacantly, almost thoughtfully, looking up, the rain dripping from his grizzled head, and rivulets of water trickling about his shoes.

"Hello, Uncle Dick," said the messenger. "Enjoying the prospect? River's risin'; better come back with me."

But the old man only answered, "Johnson? Not here! Nickols? Not here!

Bemis? Not here! Bradley? Not here! Hicks? Not here! And Barringer? Here! And now God's moved the rain belt west. Moved it so far west that there's hope for Lazarus to get irrigation from Abraham.''

And with this the old man went into the house. There, when the five days' rain had ceased, and when the great river that flooded the barren plain had shrunk, the rescuing party, coming from Maize, found him. Beside his bed were his balanced books and his legal papers. In his dead eyes were a thousand dreams.

The Prodigal Daughter

Folks like to pamper the prodigal son
—Maybe no more than they'd orter—
But no one as yet has been able to get
Any veal for his prodigal daughter.
From the Rhymed Reflections of Elder Twiggs.

A FEW years ago the Beasly girl worked in the over-all factory. She was a pretty girl then, and naturally the neighbors talked about her, for the people who live along Jersey Creek are really no better than they who live on Independence Avenue, in spite of the theories that poverty and charity go together. So when she left the factory the women of the Jersey Creek neighborhood hinted that the foreman had been too polite to her. But if she had remained at the factory they would have given the same reason for her staying. After that, she went to the theatre with young men who turned up their coat collars

and wore their hands in their pockets in the
fall and spring, in lieu of overcoats. During
the summer following her discharge from the
over-all factory she became a park fiend.

When she gave up her counter in the
cheap dry-goods store, she remained at
home, apparently keeping house for her
father. He worked in "the shops" somewhere over in "the bottoms," and came
home tired and grimy at night, and went to
bed early. He slept in the room off the
kitchen, and his daughter slept in the front
room. He did not know when she came in
at night, and he did not think of caring to
know. Her father paid no attention to the
little brother and sister who teased the
daughter at table about the young men who
frequented the house. If the other members of the family had been plaguing the
ten-year old girl who led in the raillery, the
father would have been equally heedless of
their chatter. The eldest daughter made
him very happy by simple tendernesses,
though, of course, he did not understand
that his warmth for her and the longing

which he felt all day to get home for supper, was happiness.

But, unconsciously, his daughter grew very
necessary to him. He was not of the world
that analyzes its emotions, yet he could not
fail to see her beauty, nor to be proud of her
for it; and when she was dressed to go
out—and she went out early and often—his
pride blinded him to the gaudiness of her
clothes, her frowsy hair, and the shocking
make-up on her pretty face. Probably his
discernment was not keen enough to see
these faults, even had he not been so fond
of her. But other fathers who had daughters saw these things, and mothers of the
neighborhood who had sons did not mention
the Beasly girl in the family circle. It was
only after Miss Beasly had joined a Comedy
Company, organized to play the "White
Slave" and "Only a Farmer's Daughter"
through the West, that her name was mentioned at all freely by Jersey Creek's aristocracy, and then it was as if she were dead.
And Mrs. Hinkley, who took care of the
children and looked after the lonely old

man, often said to inquiring women of the
neighborhood, "It would break your heart
to see Mr. Beasly a-grievin' an' a-grievin'
for that hussy; an' whiniver he gets a letter
from her he reads it at the supper table before them children wid that flourish you 'd
think —tch, tch, tch, I do wonder if he
knows." And after some discussion she
would sigh, "Well, it's not for me to tell
him."

What a wonderful thing is absence. It is
like the dark in its power to transform people and situations and the relations of things.
Though she had grown up under his eyes,
the old man and his daughter had scarcely
spoken a serious word to each other. The
father had never inquired what his daughter
was or was not. She was only "her" in his
thoughts. They were strangers, but when
he began to forget her presence, he found
himself continually thinking of things he
would like to say to her. "Her" disappeared, and dreams altogether different from
his former conception of her, took her place.
He longed for her, and yearned to tell her

the great love in his heart. Among the noisy wheels, he mumbled to himself, speeches that he wanted to make to her, and in the scrawled letter he sent her occasionally, he wrote some of these tender things.

One day she wrote that she was coming home for a vacation, and his heart was very glad. He read and re-read the letter, and droned it off at the supper table to Mrs. Hinkley and the children. As he read it, neither the hearers nor the reader realized how much feeling the writer had put into the matter-of-fact words, "I want to be home with you all again." These words were meant to tell a story of heart-ache and loneliness and despair, but they were commonplace and fell short. For poor people are as blunt in sensibility as the comfortably rich, and the suggestion to Mrs. Hinkley of the possibility of any human feeling in the Beasly girl's heart would have fallen on barren soil.

When the day for the girl's coming arrived, Mrs. Hinkley was gone from the Beasly home, but the old man had "laid off" a day from his work. He was joyful in the hope that he might say some of the tender things he had written, and then keep up the new happiness that had come to him, yet he feared that his daughter would be so far above him that she would not care for it. He put on his best suit of clothes, and sent the children away. The house was in conspicuous "company order;" he arranged things, himself, and a Sunday stiffness and quiet prevailed. He sat in the front room waiting for her. When he heard voices at the fence, he recognized that of his daughter, and his pulse quickened; but when he looked through the curtain and saw a stranger with her, his heart sank.

Father and daughter met at the door; he held out his hand to her and she passed in, followed by the stranger, while the father said awkwardly, "Well, Allie,"—and after a pause, "how are you?"

A smile enclosed the commonplace answer, and the old man continued in a high-keyed tone with the upward inflection, looking vacantly at the dapper stranger who had not been introduced, "I s 'pose you 've been gettin' to be such a grand lady—" He laughed nervously, and with conscious embarrassment. The daughter seated her guest, and the father, with a feint at cheer, chirped, "Well, you 're lookin' hale and hearty."

"Is there anything in the cupboard, Pa?" asked the girl, as she took off her soiled gloves and threw her long, shabby cloak and her expensive, but betowsled hat upon the bed. "I am just dyin' for a bite; we didn't get any breakfast." The old man went to get something, and when he returned the stranger was gone. She did not taste what he had brought, but turned and threw her arms about his neck; there were tears in her eyes as she said, "Oh, Pa—Pa—ain't it good to be back again!"

The father, summoning all his courage to break away from the common words of welcome began again in a quavering, nervous voice, "Well, Allie—I guess 'at mebbe you —you think someway that yer daddy has forgot you, but — Allie, I tell you, I—well,

do you know, I think a whole lot of you,
Allie.'' It was the best he could do, but
he kissed her, and that was something—it
was a great deal for both of them. Then
they relaxed, and talked of the children,
about whom she asked a great deal, and
of the neighbors, about whom she asked
nothing.

The ''Comedy Company'' had failed, and
she was at home to stay. Her absence had
made both father and daughter understand
how much each was to the other. The little
signs of endearment did not vanish as the
days wore on. She smoothed his hair when
she passed him, and he caught at her dress
and touched her simply with his hand as she
came near him at her work. So much was
his heart wrapped up in her that he did not
notice the absence of the neighbors from the
house, and when he asked them to come, and
laughingly upbraided them for their social
carelessness, he accepted their explanations
with no thought of their insincerity.

His pride in her knew no conventionality
and no propriety. Once, when the boys in

the shop were eating their noonday lunch in
the shade of the building, he looked up from
a piece of pie to say in a lull of the conversation, "You fellers may talk all you want to
about your purty girls, but I bet I 've got
one at home 'at 'l beat all yours put together. Some o' you young fellers orto
come out an' see her." And when the fellows winked at one another and set up a
laugh, the old man laughed, too, and said,
"That's what I said; and I did n't smile
when I said it; she 's the purtiest girl you
ever saw—ef her dad does say so."

He told her that night how they had
laughed, and how he had "stuck to his
words and made them shut up," but she was
bending over the stove in the dark corner,
and he could not see the flash in her eyes,
and the quick quiver of hate that curled the
muscles of her upper lip. The old man and
the children prattled on until she composed
herself, and joined the family group.

That night she tossed in her bed and
turned her feverish pillow a hundred times.
She cursed the world, its people, and its

social arrangement. She wanted to make
people suffer. Her father's disgrace, and
the thought that she could not defend him
made her frantic. When it was nearly morning she cried herself to sleep, brooding over
her own personal sorrow. She was awakened by her father scraping the ashes from
the kitchen stove, and her heart rose to her
throat with great love for him. During that
entire day the girl held her father in her
mind as she went about her household du-
ties. It seemed to her that her life with him
was really worth living, and she was glad
that since her return, she had sent her old
companions away. Yet her hand was raised
against the world—her narrow world that is
the epitome of the great narrow world—because it persecuted her and pointed its finger
at the one being she loved. But the very
fact that her father was set apart from his
fellows because of her, drew him close to her.
And the night thoughts followed her all
through the day, till she longed for his return.
It was a good day in her life.

She heard his footsteps on the walk in

front, and heard him coming around the house to the kitchen door. When he crossed the threshold she kissed him. The old man was a little abashed at the suddenness of it, but he was pleased. He took a chair and sat in the back yard leaning against the house. From there he talked with her through the open door. They had passed the usual questions of the day, when the old man said, "Allie, y' can't guess what Mrs. Hinkley said about you, this evening." The daughter blanched as she stood in the doorway, and said nothing. It was dusk, and the old man did not notice her. "She said, sez she, ' Mr. Beasly, do you know that you are doin' wrong to keep that Allie in the house there?' I says, 'Why so, Mrs. Hinkley?' and she would n't say nothin' but 'Well, y' are, that's all.' I s'pose Mrs. Hinkley thinks that 'cause you 're grown to be so purty an'—an' all that—you 're ashamed to stay down here in Jersey with your old daddy." Strange things were crowding into the girl's mind — a fearful impulse to unburden her soul struggled for mastery in her heart. Then the temptation came with her father's question, "But you ain't ashamed to stay with your poor, honest ol' pap, are y', Allie?"

There was a short silence. As it lengthened into a distinct pause the man's heart was shot with fear. He felt remorse wrap him about — remorse and humiliation. He sprang lamely from the leaning chair to his feet and staggered to the door, crying piteously with woe in his voice, "Oh, Allie, Allie — my — my little girl, Allie! We 'll move, Allie; we 'll move."

He came to her and stood helplessly before her. He could not know why she was dumb. He misunderstood and was turning away in a slow agony of shame, when her love for him swept her as upon a wave into his arms, sobbing.

She recovered quickly, and hastened to a sputtering pan which she pretended needed her attention. The old man touched her dress in his wonted way, as he passed her going toward the door. He hesitated, and seemed to have another protest upon his lips. The daughter felt that she could not keep her sorrow back if he spoke. The old man did not note the pathetic tremble in her voice as she cried to her little sister, playing at the door:

"Jen-nee, Jennie, o-o-h Jennie, you go cut me a switch; I got to tend to your Pa. He's makin' me spoil this supper." She added in a firmer voice. "The very idee of our movin'."

And the old man, looking back with a smile, went into the twilight full of joy.

The Record on the Blotter

THE old man Beasly went over the whole matter to the big wheel that day, and the big wheel murmured a low, monotonous affirmative to everything he said. She had been a good daughter to him, he said, and the wheel assented; she had been more thoughtful of him, since she came back from the stranded theatrical company, than ever before, and the wheel mumbled its belief that this was true; she had stayed at home every night since she came back, and the wheel whirred sympathetically; she had added many bright touches to the little shanty on Jersey Creek, and the wheel rolled back no denial; why then should they say these things, he asked. "Why?" snarled the wheel,—what if she had enjoyed the things young girls enjoy, pretty clothes, buggy rides, and the attentions of

young men; do not other girls have these
things? "They do," growled the wheel, as
it struggled with the belt; then is she worse
than other girls because she had no mother,
he concluded, and "No, no, no," moaned the
wheel in a constant torrent of wrath against
the world—the old man's little world that
was organized against his daughter—so that
he was in a frenzy at it, and cursed it and its
figure heads, who had told him, not in hints,
but bluntly, that his daughter could not stay
in the Jersey Creek neighborhood. The
wheel ground the anger into his soul as he
stood at his bench beside it; at lunch time
he kept apart from the men in the shops and
barely tasted his food. The thought of
what Mrs. Hinkley had said to him as he
passed her house that morning going to his
work, inflamed him, and it seemed a wonder
to him that he could stand there so dumbly
and listen, without rage, and without utter-
ing one resentful syllable, until she had
closed her door behind her. How he longed
to fly at her, and what a fury of words
burned on his tongue as the hours dragged

on, and he mumbled incoherent, passionate phrases to the wheel.

As soon as the children were on the streets and the men well out of the houses, the women of the Jersey Creek neighborhood knew what Mrs. Hinkley had done. She told how Mr. Beasly, shame-faced and speechless, had listened to her protest against letting the girl remain in the honest neighborhood, and the women, mistaking his dumb surprise for a confession of guilt, let their indignation carry them to a point where it was decided that Mrs. Hinkley should go to the Beasly house and tell the daughter what had been said to her father.

So, early in the afternoon, Mrs. Hinkley started on her errand. When the task was done, Mrs. Hinkley went straight to a neighbor's house, where two or three women were gathered to hear her report.

"Well, I done it," she said, as she sank into a rocking chair. "I did n't waste no words, but just up and told her how we all knowed about her carryin's on, and how she'd got to go where she belonged, and

how her pap knowed it, and how he just as
good as said he 'd see she went. Oh, I guess
she won't flounce 'round here in her fine
rags much more. Say? Why, bless you,
what could she say? She didn't say
nothin'; did n't even whimper, the brazen
thing, at my tellin' her how her old pap
hung his head and sneaked off when I faced
him with her wickedness. And as they
was nothin' else to say and she did n't want
to argie, I got up and left."

The wheel may have told the old man
something of this, for it groaned and wailed
and howled in agony that afternoon, until
the workman's nerves were frayed and tattered by its lashings. At three o'clock he
could stand it no longer, and he let the
foreman put a substitute at his bench. During the half hour which he spent hurrying
homeward, a thousand horrible fancies filled
his brain. What if his motherless girl had
been wayward, he thought, and then hated
himself for thinking so. He saw, in the
fever heat of his excitement, all the unno-
ticed carelessness of his course toward her;

it flashed across his mind that he had al-
lowed her to choose her own companions,
and then he thought with horror of the big
city beyond Jersey Creek. But a warm
flush of tenderness came over him at the
recollection of her gentleness; the hundred
little caresses which she threw to him in
passing, while at her work, erased his self-
condemnation and thrilled him with happiness. The grim workingman was thinking as does a drunken man, reasoning
with the syllogism of a delirium. A train
thundered by as he passed Mrs. Hinkley's
house. He met her at her door. She said
something he did not hear for the crashing
train. An instinctive fear that she had been
taunting his daughter quickened his pace
to a trot.

The house was quiet, the dark blue cam-
bric curtains were down. The thought of
his poor girl suffering from the woman's
cruel taunts frenzied him. As he ran around
the house there was no thought of anything
save his daughter's innocence in his mind.
All her goodness rose before him as he

darted in the back door.   He did not con-
nect the presence of a pungent smoke in the
kitchen with anything at all, but pressed
on to the front room.

It was a minute—sixty throbbing ages—
before he realized it all.   Then he recalled
the face of the taunting woman in the street.
He instinctively knew what she had said,
and in the very tension of his nerves, his
iron frame was rigid and his pulse seemed
calm.   He did not break, and his eyes,
which in cool hate saw only the taunting face,
were not soothed by tears.   He knew, with
a wisdom wiser than his own simple deduc-
tion, that the taunting lips would call his
daughter's death confession.   Then he saw
that she had done it to save him from the
very disgrace she was bringing upon herself.
He was conscious for the first time of the
pungent odor of the smoke.   He picked up
the pistol which still smelled strongly of the
burned powder.   There was one load gone,
and the tempter came as he looked at the
loaded cylinders.   Then, in a burst of lurid,
unhealthy light that came, as he saw that

his death would only attest his child's disgrace, he formed a plan for denying her confession to the world and to the taunting
face.   The jolting processes of his brain were
being moved by a power that came from
the jarring, broken logic of a dream.

In another hour this power had welded
into fact, the grotesque resolution of his
dream.   The record on the captain's blotter
at the station read:

"John Beasly, aged 60.   Held for the
murder of Alice Beasly, his daughter.   Con-
fessed to the captain in charge."

The King of Boyville

BOYS who are born in a small town are born free and equal. In the big city it may be different; there are doubtless good little boys who disdain bad little boys, and poor little boys who are never to be noticed under any circumstances. But in a small town, every boy, good or bad, rich or poor, stands among boys on his own merits. The son of the banker who owns a turning-pole in the back yard, does homage to the baker's boy who can sit on the bar and drop and catch by his legs; while the good little boy who is kept in wide collars and cuffs by a mistaken mother, gazes through the white paling of his father's fence at the troop headed for the swimming hole, and pays all the reverence which his dwarfed nature can muster to the sign of the two fingers. In the social order of boys who live in country towns, a boy is measured by what he can do, and not by what his father is. And so, Winfield Hancock Pennington, whose boy name was Piggy Pennington, was the King of Boyville. For Piggy could walk on his hands, curling one foot gracefully over his back, and pointing the other straight in the air; he could hang by his heels on a fly-ing trapeze; he could chin a pole so many times that no one could count the number; he could turn a somersault in the air from the level ground, both backwards and for-wards, he could "tread" water and "lay" his hair; he could hit any marble in any ring from "taws" and "knucks down,"—and bet-ter than all, he could cut his initials in the ice on skates, and whirl around and around so many times that he looked like an ani-mated shadow, when he would dart away up the stream, his red "comfort" flapping be-hind him like a laugh of defiance. In the story books such a boy would be the son of a widowed mother, and turn out very good or very bad, but Piggy was not a story book boy, and his father kept a grocery store, from

which Piggy used to steal so many dates that
the boys said his father must have cut up
the almanac to supply him. As he never
gave the goodies to the other boys, but kept
them for his own use, his name of "Piggy"
was his by all the rights of Boyville.

There was one thing Piggy Pennington
could not do, and it was the one of all
things which he most wished he could do;
he could not under any circumstances say
three consecutive and coherent words to any
girl under fifteen and over nine. He was
invited with nearly all of the boys of his age
in town, to children's parties. And while
any other boy, whose only accomplishment
was turning a cart wheel, or skinning the
cat backwards, or, at most, hanging by one
leg and turning a handspring, could boldly
ask a girl if he could see her home, Piggy
had to get his hat and sneak out of the
house when the company broke up. He
would comfort himself by walking along on
the opposite side of the street from some
couple, while he talked in monosyllables
about a joke which he and the boy knew,

but which was always a secret to the girl.
Even after school Piggy could not join the
select coterie of boys who followed the girls
down through town to the postoffice. He
could not tease the girls about absent boys
at such times and make up rhymes like

"First the cat and then her tail;
Jimmy Sears and Maggie Hale,"

and shout them out for the crowd to hear.
Instead of joining this courtly troupe Piggy
Pennington went off with the boys who
really did n't care for such things, and
fought, or played "tracks up," or wrestled
his way leisurely home in time to get in
his "night wood." But his heart was not
in these pastimes; it was with a red shawl
of a peculiar shade, that was wending its
way to the postoffice and back to a home in
one of the few two-story houses in the little
town. Time and again had Piggy tried to
make some sign to let his feelings be known,
but every time he had failed. Lying in
wait for her at corners, and suddenly breaking upon her with a glory of backward and
forward somersaults did not convey the state

of his heart.   Hanging by his heels from an apple tree limb over the sidewalk in front of her, unexpectedly, did not tell the tender tale for which his lips could find no words.   And the nearest he could come to an expression of the longing in his breast, was to cut her initials in the ice beside his own when she came weaving and wobbling past on some other boy's arm.   But she would not look at the initials, and the chirography of his skates was so indistinct that it required a key; and everything put together, poor Piggy was no nearer a declaration at the end of the winter than he had been at the beginning of autumn.   So only one heart beat with but a single thought, and the other took motto candy and valentines and red apples and picture cards and other tokens of esteem from other boys, and beat on with any number of thoughts, entirely immaterial to the uses of this narrative.   But Piggy Pennington did not take to the enchantment of corn silk cigarettes and rattan and grape vine cigars; he tried to sing, and wailed dismal ballads about the "Gypsy's Warning," and

"The Child in the Grave With Its Mother,"
and "She's a Daisy, She's a Darling,
She's a Dumpling, She's a Lamb," when-
ever he was in hearing distance of his Heart's
Desire, in the hope of conveying to her
some hint of the state of his affections;
but it was useless. Even when he tried to
whistle plaintively as he passed her house
in the gloaming, his notes brought forth no
responsive echo.

One morning in the late spring, he spent
half an hour before breakfast among his
mother's roses, which were just in first
bloom. He had taken out there all the
wire from an old broom, and all his kite
string. His mother had to call three times
before he would leave his work. The
youngster was the first to leave the table,
and by eight o'clock he was at his task again.
Before the first school bell had rung, Piggy
Pennington was bound for the school house
with a strange looking parcel under his arm.
He tried to put his coat over it, but it stuck
out and the newspaper ·that was wrapped
around it, bulged into so many corners,

that it looked like a home-tied bundle of laundry.

"What you got?" asked the freckle-faced boy, who was learning at Piggy's feet how to do the "muscle grind" on the turn-ing-pole.

But Piggy Pennington was the King of Boyville, and he had a right to look straight ahead of him, as if he did not hear the question, and say:

"Lookie here, Mealy, I wish you would go and tell Abe I want him to hurry up, for I want to see him."

"Abe" was Piggy's nearest friend. His other name was Carpenter. Piggy only wished to be rid of the freckle-faced boy. But the freckle-faced boy was not used to royalty and its ways, so he pushed his in-quiry.

"Say, Piggy, have you got your red ball-pants in that bundle?"

There was no reply. The freckle-faced boy grew tired of tatooing with a stick, as they walked beside a paling fence, so he be-gan touching every tree on the other side of the path with his fingers. They had gone a block when the freckle-faced boy could stand it no longer and said:

"Say Piggy, you need n't be so smart about your old bundle; now honest, Piggy, what have you got in that bundle?"

"Aw — soft soap, take a bite — good fer yer appetite," said the King, as he faced about and drew up his left cheek and lower eye-lid pugnaciously. The freckle-faced boy saw he would have to fight if he stayed, so he turned to go, and said, as though nothing had happened, "Where do you suppose old Abe is, anyhow?"

Just before school was called Piggy Pennington was playing "scrub" with all his might, and a little girl—his Heart's Desire— was taking out of her desk a wreath of roses, tied to a shaky wire frame. There was a crowd of girls around her admiring it, and speculating about the possible author of the gift; but to these she did not show the patent medicine card, on which was scrawled, over the druggist's advertisement:

"Yours truly, W. H. P."

When the last bell rang, Piggy Pennington was the last boy in, and he did not look toward the desk, where he had put the flowers, until after the singing.

Then he stole a sidewise glance that way, and his Heart's Desire was deep in her geography. It was an age before she filed past him with the "B" class in geography, and took a seat directly in front of him, where he could look at her all the time, unobserved by her. Once she squirmed in her place and looked toward him, but Piggy Pennington was head over heels in the "Iser rolling rapidly." When their eyes did at last meet, just as Piggy, leading the marching around the room, was at the door to go out for recess, the thrill amounted to a shock that sent him whirling in a pin wheel of handsprings toward the ball ground, shouting "scrub — first bat, first bat, first bat," from sheer, bubbling joy. Piggy made four tallies that recess, and the other boys could n't have put him out, if they had used a hand-grenade or a Babcock fire extinguisher.

He received four distinct shots that day
from the eyes of his Heart's Desire, and the
last one sent him home on the run, tripping
up every primary urchin, whom he found
tagging along by the way, and whooping at
the top of his voice.   When his friends met
in his barn, some fifteen minutes later, Piggy
tried to turn a double somersault from his
spring board, to the admiration of the
crowd, and was only calmed by falling with
his full weight on his head and shoulders at
the edge of the hay, with the life nearly
jolted out of his little body.

The next morning, Piggy Pennington as-
tonished his friends by bringing a big armful
of réd and yellow and pink and white roses
to school.

He had never done this before, and when
he had run the gauntlet of the big boys,
who were not afraid to steal them from him,
he made straight for his schoolroom, and
stood holding them in his hands while the
girls gathered about him teasing for the
beauties.   It was nearly time for the last
bell to ring, and Piggy knew that his Heart's

Desire would be in the room by the time
he got there. He was not mistaken. But
Heart's Desire did not clamor with the other
girls for one of the roses. Piggy stood off
their pleadings as 'long as he could with
"Naw," "Why naw, of course I won't,"
"Naw, what I want to give you one for,"
and "Go way from here I tell you," and
still Heart's Desire did not ask for her flowers. There were but a few moments left
before school would be called to order, and
in desperation Piggy gave one rose away.
It was not a very pretty rose, but he hoped
she would see that the others were to be given
away, and ask for one. But she — his Heart's
Desire — stood near a window, talking to the
freckle-faced boy. Then Piggy gave away
one rose after another. As the last bell began to ring he gave them to the boys, as
the girls were all supplied. And still she
came not. There was one rose left, the
most beautiful of all. She went to her desk,
and as the teacher came in, bell in hand,
Piggy surprised himself, the teacher, and
the school by laying the beautiful flower,

without a word on the teacher's desk. That
day was a dark day. When a new boy, who
did n't belong to the school, came up at recess to play, Piggy shuffled over to him and
asked gruffly:

"What 's your name?"

"Puddin' 'n' tame, ast me agin an' I 'll
tell you the same," said the new boy, and
then there was a fight. It did n't sooth
Piggy's feelings one bit that he whipped the
new boy, for the new boy was smaller than
Piggy. And he dared not turn his flushed
face towards his Heart's Desire. It was
almost four o'clock when Piggy Pennington
walked to the master's desk to get him to
work out a problem, and as he passed the
desk of Heart's Desire he dropped a note
in her lap. It read:

"Are you mad?"

But he dared not look for the answer, as
they marched out that night, so he contented himself with punching the boy ahead
of him with a pin, and stepping on his heels,
when they were in the back part of the room,
where the teacher would not see him. The

King of Boyville walked home alone that
evening. The courtiers saw plainly that his
majesty was troubled.

So his lonely way was strewn with broken
stick-horses, which he took from the little
boys, and was marked by trees adorned with
the string, which he took from other young-
sters, who ran across his pathway playing
horse. In his barn he sat listlessly on a
nail keg, while Abe and the freckle-faced boy
did their deeds of daring, on the rings, and
the trapeze. Only when the new boy came
in, did Piggy arouse himself to mount the
flying bar, and, swinging in it to the very raf-
ters, drop and hang by his knees, and again
drop from his knees, catching his ankle in
the angle of the rope where it meets the
swinging bar. That was to awe the new boy.

After this feat the King was quiet.

At dusk, when the evening chores were
done, Piggy Pennington walked past the
home of his Heart's Desire and howled out
a doleful ballad which began:

" You ask what makes this darkey wee -eep,
    Why he like others am not gay."

But a man on the sidewalk passing said, "Well son, that's pretty good, but wouldn't you just as lief sing as to make that noise." So the King went to bed with a heavy heart.

He took that heart to school with him, the next morning, and dragged it over the school ground, playing crack the whip and "stink-base." But when he saw Heart's Desire wearing in her hair one of the white roses from his mother's garden—the Pennington's had the only white roses in the little town— he knew it was from the wreath which he had given her, and so light was his boyish heart, that it was with an effort that he kept it out of his throat. There were smiles and smiles that day. During the singing they began, and every time she came past him from a class, and every time he could pry his eyes behind her geography, or her grammar, a flood of gladness swept over his soul. That night Piggy Pennington followed the girls from the schoolhouse to the postoffice, and in a burst of enthusiasm, he walked on his hands in front of the crowd, for nearly half a block. When his Heart's Desire said:

"O ain't you afraid you 'll hurt yourself, doing that?'' Piggy pretended not to hear her, and said to the boys:

"Aw, that ain't nothin'; come down to my barn, an' I 'll do somepin that'll make yer head swim."

He was too exuberant to contain himself, and when he left the girls he started to run after a stray chicken, that happened along, and ran till he was out of breath. He did not mean to run in the direction his Heart's Desire had taken, but he turned a corner, and came up with her suddenly.

Her eyes beamed upon him, and he could not run away, as he wished. She made room for him on the sidewalk, and he could do nothing but walk beside her. For a block they were so embarrassed that neither spoke.

It was Piggy who broke the silence. His words came from his heart. He had not yet learned to speak otherwise.

"Where 's your rose?" he asked, not seeing it.

"What rose?" said the girl, as though she

had never in her short life heard of such an absurd thing as a rose.

"Oh, you know," returned the boy, stepping irregularly, to make the tips of his toes come on the cracks in the sidewalk.   There was another pause, during which Piggy picked up a pebble, and threw it at a bird in a tree.   His heart was sinking rapidly.

"O, that rose?" said his Heart's Desire, turning full upon him with the enchantment of her childish eyes. "Why, here it is in my grammar.   I 'm taking it to keep with the others.   Why?"

"O, nuthin' much," replied the boy. "I bet you can't do this," he added, as he glowed up into her eyes from an impulsive handspring.

And thus the King of Boyville first set his light, little foot upon the soil of an unknown country.

A Story of The Highlands

CROSSING the Missouri river into Kansas, the west-bound traveler begins a steady, upward climb, until he reaches the summit of the Rockies. The journey through Kansas covers in four hundred miles nearly five thousand feet of the long, upward slant. In that long hillside there are three or four distinct kinds of landscape, distinguished from one another by the trees that trim the horizon.

The hills and bluffs that roll away from the river are covered with scrub oaks, elms, walnuts, and sycamores. As the wayfarer pushes westward, the oak drops back, then the sycamore follows the walnut, and finally the elm disappears, until three hundred miles to the westward, the horizon of the "gently rolling" prairie is serrated by the scraggy cottonwood, that rises awkwardly by some sandbarred stream, oozing over the moundy land. Another fifty miles, and at Garden City, high up on the background of the panorama, even the cottonwood staggers; and here and there, around some sink-hole in the great flat floor of the prairie, droops a desolate willow—the last weary pilgrim from the lowlands.

When the traveler has mounted to this high table land, nearly four hundred miles from the Missouri, he may walk for days without seeing any green thing higher than his head. He may journey for hours on horseback, and not climb a hill, seeing before him only the level and often barren plain, scarred now and then by irrigation ditches.

The even line of the horizon is seldom marred. The silence of such a scene gnaws the glamour from the heart. Men become harsh and hard; women grow withered and sodden under its blighting power. The song of wood birds is not heard; even the mournful plaint of the meadow lark loses its sentiment, where the dreary clanking drone of the wind-mill is the one song which really brings good tidings with it. Long and fiercely sounds this unrhythmical monody in the night, when the traveler lies down to rest in the little sun-burned, pine-board town. The gaunt arms of the wheel hurl its imprecations at him as he rises to resume his journey into the silence, under the great gray dome, with its canopy pegged tightly down about him everywhere.

Crops are as bountiful in Kansas as elsewhere on the globe. It is the constant cry for aid, coming from this plateau—only a small part of the state—which reaches the world's ears, and the world blames Kansas. The fair springs on these highlands lure home-seekers to their ruin.

Hundreds of men and women have been tempted to death or worse, by this Lorelei of the prairies.

A young man named Burkholder came out to Fountain county in 1885. He had been a well-to-do young fellow in Illinois, was a graduate of an inland college, a man of good judgment, of sense, of a well-arranged mental perspective. In 1885 money was plentiful. He stocked his farm, put on a mortgage, and brought a wife back from the home of his boyhood. She was a young woman of culture, who put a bookshelf in the corner of the best of the three rooms in the yellow pine shanty, in which she and her husband lived. She brought her upright piano, and adorned her bed-room floor with bright rugs. She bought magazines at the "Post Office Book Store" of the prairie town. She was not despondent. The vast stretches of green cheered her through the hot summer. There was a novel fascination in the wide, treeless horizon which charmed her for a while. At first she never tired of glancing up from her work, through the south window of the kitchen, to see the level green stretches, and the road that merged into the distance. She sat in the shade of the house, and wrote home cheerful, rollicking letters. As for roughing it, she enjoyed it thoroughly.

The crops did not quite pay the expenses of the year; so "Thomas Burkholder and

Lizzie his wife'' put another mortgage on the
farm.   The books and magazines from home
still adorned the best room.   And all through
the winter and spring, the prevailing spirits of the community buoyed up the young
people.   It was during the summer of
1887 that the first hot winds came.   They
blighted everything.   The kaffir corn, the
grass, the dust-laden weeds by the wayside
curled up under their fiery breath from
the southwestern desert.   Mrs. Burkholder
stayed indoors.   The dust spread itself over
everything.   It came into the house like a
flood, pouring through the loose window
frames and weather-boarding.   Mrs. Burkholder, looking out of her window on these
days, could see only a great dust dragon,
writhing up and down the brown road and
over the prairie for miles and miles.   The
scene seemed weirdly dry.   She found
herself longing, one day, for a fleck of
water in the landscape.   That longing grew
upon her.   She said nothing of it, but in
her day dreams there was always a mental
itching to put water into the lustreless pic-

ture framed by her kitchen window.   It was a kind of soul thirst.   In one of her letters she wrote:

"The hot winds have killed everything this year, but most of all I grieve for the little cottonwood saplings on the 'eighty' in front of the house.   There is not a tree anywhere in sight, and as the government requires that we should plant trees on our place, as a partial payment for it, I was so in hopes that these would do well.   They are burned up now.   You do n't know how lonesome it seems without trees."

She did not tell the home folk that her piano and the books had gone to buy provisions for the winter.   She did not tell the home folk that she had not bought a new dress since she left Illinois.   She did not let her petty cares burden her letter.   She wrote of generalities.   "You do not know how I miss the hills.   Tom and I rode twenty miles yesterday, to a place called the Taylor Bottom.   It is a deep sink-hole, perhaps fifty feet deep, containing about ten square acres.   By getting down into this we

have the effect of hills.   You cannot know
how good and snug, and tucked in and
'comfy' it seemed.   It is so naked at the
house with the knife-edge on the horizon,
and only the sky over you.   Tom and I
have been busy.   I have n't had time to
read the story in the magazine you sent me.
Tom can't get corduroys out here.   You
should see him in overalls."

Mrs. Burkholder helped her husband look
after the cattle.   The hired man went away
in the early fall.   This she did not write
home either.   All through the winter days
she heard the keen wind whistle around the
house, and when she was alone a dread
blanched her face.   The great gray dome
seemed to be holding her its prisoner.   She
felt chained under it. She shut her eyes and
strove to get away from it in fancy, to think
of green hills and woodland; but her eyes
tore themselves open, and with a hypnotic
terror she went to the window, where the
prairie thrall bound her again in its chains.

The cemetery for the prairie town had
been started during the spring before, and

some one had planted therein a solitary cottonwood sapling. Its two dead, gaunt
branches seemed to be beckoning her, and
all day she thought she heard the winds
shriek through the new iron fences around
the graves and through the grass that grew
wild about the dead. The scene haunted
her. It was for this end that the gray dome
held her, she thought, as she listened during
the cold nights to the hard, dry snow as it
beat against the board shanty wherein she
lay awake.

In the spring the mover's caravan filed by
the house, starting eastward before planting
time. When the train of wagons had passed
the year before, Mrs. Burkholder had been
amused by the fantastic legends, which the
wagon covers—white, clean, prosperous—
had borne. "Kansas or bust," they used
to read when headed westward. "Busted"
was the laconic legend, written under the old
motto on their first eastward trip. "Going
back to wife's folks," had been a common
jocose motto at first. Mrs. Burkholder
and her husband had laughed over this

the year before, but this year as she
saw the long line file out of the west
into the east, she missed the banners. She
noticed, with a mental pang, that those who
came out of the country this year seemed
to be thankful to get out at all. There
were times when she had to struggle to con-
ceal her cowardice; for she wished to turn
away from the fright, to flee from the gray
dome, and from the beckoning of the dead
cottonwood in the graveyard.

The spring slipped away, and another sul-
try summer came on, and then a long,
dry fall. Mrs. Burkholder and her husband worked together.

There were whole weeks when she neg-
lected her toilet; she tried to brighten up
in the evening, and dutifully went at the
magazines that were regularly sent to her by
the home folks.

But she seemed to need sleep, and the
cares of the day weighed upon her. The
interests of the world of culture grew small
in her vision. The work before her
seemed to demand all her thought; so that

serial after serial slipped through the magazines unread, and new literary men and fads
rose and fell, all unknown to her. The pile
of magazines at the foot of the bed grew
dustier every day.

The Burkholders got their share of the
seed-grain sent to Fountain county by the
Kansas Legislature, and just after planting
time in 1889, the land was gloriously green.
But before July, the promises had been
mocked by the hiss of the hot wind in the
dead grass. That fall one of their horses
died.

Saturday after Saturday, Burkholder went
to the prairie town and brought home gro-
ceries and coal. It was a source of constant
terror to him that some day his wife might
ask how he got these supplies. She hid it
from herself as long as she could. All winter they would not admit to each other that
they were living on "aid." On many a
gray, blustering afternoon, when Burkholder
was in the village getting provisions, a strag-
gler on the road might see his wife
coming around the house, with two buckets

of water in her hands, the water splashing against her feet, which were encased in a pair of her husband's old shoes, the wind pushing her thin calico skirts against her limbs, and her frail body bent stiffly in the man's coat that she wore. Her arms and shoulders seemed to shiver and crouch with the cold, and her blue features were so drawn that her friendly smile at the wayfarer was only a grimace.

In the spring many men in Fountain county went East looking for work. They left their wives with God and the county commissioners. Burkholder dumbly went with them. In March, the covered wagon train began to file past the Burkholder house. By April it was a continuous line—shabby, tattered, rickety, dying. Here came a wagon covered with bed quilts, there another topped with oil-cloth table covers; another followed, patched with everything. For two years, the mover's caravan trailing across the plains had taken the shape of a huge dust-colored serpent in the woman's fancy; now it seemed to Mrs. Burkholder that the terrible creature was withering away, that this was its skeleton. The treeless landscape worried her more and more; the steel dome seemed set tighter over her, and she sat thirsting for water in the landscape.

After a month's communion with her fancies, Mrs. Burkholder nailed a black rag over the kitchen window. But the arms of the dead sapling in the cemetery gyrated wildly in her sick imagination. It was a long summer, and when it was done, there was one more vacant house, one more among hundreds far out on the highlands. There is one more mound in the bleak country graveyard, where the wind, shrieking through the iron fences and the crackling, dead cottonwood branches, has never learned a slumber song to sob for a tired soul. But there are times when the wind seems to moan upon its sun-parched chords like the cry of some lone spirit groping its tangled way back to the lowlands, the green pastures, the still waters, and to the peace that passeth understanding.

"The Fraud of Men"

IT was in the reception room of a club house in an inland city, where the two young men had met by chance that evening. There was a stuffy profusion of leather furniture in the room that gave it a heavy cast. A long dark table was covered with papers fastened in automatic wooden holders. The presence of the table indicated that the club was economizing space by combining reception room and reading room. The firm grip of the wooden paper-holder gave rise to the suspicion that some one might sell his honor for a nickel and walk off with the papers. In the club-room, men were talking in knots of two or three, apparently on business, and when an outsider entered a group, conversation was distinctly and painfully suspended, or lagged in cold formalities until he had drifted away. The men there were clearly business

men, and were there by business appoint-
ment, and the element of sociability was
manifest only in the click of the billiard balls
that echoed in from some invisible rear
room, where the younger men, too tired
to go to the theatre, or to the evening
gathering with their wives or sweethearts,
were walking uncounted miles after the
ivory balls. The crowd in the room was
dressed better than the crowd in the grocery store of a smaller town in the early evening. But in the club-room, adorned by
etchings of the "Angelus" and "The Nea-
politan Girl" and "The Horse Fair," the
men gathered were inspired by much the
same instincts which called the humbler
group together, and the city men were dis-
cussing affairs that differed in degree, not in
kind, from the problems which keep conversation adrift in humbler communities,— the
railroad, the bridge, the market, and the
coming election.

It was a brisk autumn evening, and the
clock on the mantel was striking eight when
two young men pulled their fat chairs to

the window, where they could see the theatre goers hurrying by under the arc light,
and where they might not be interrupted.
Their backs were turned toward the center
of the room, and they settled down among
the springs with exclamations of comfort-
able satisfaction.

"Well, old man, what d' you think of the
East," asked the shorter of the two, a very
stubby little man with a red face, red
lips and a bristling, close-cropped mustache.
His companion was a tall man with skinny
features, square shoulders, a head poised
too far back at times, but capable of bending, and he had a habit of picking at his
moustache.

"Oh, damn the East," said the tall young
man. "Jim, I 'll tell you what 's a God 's
truth, they are the worst lot of jays back
there,— absolutely the worst, that grow on
earth. They do n't know any more about
this country, and what 's in it, than a satrap
of Persia. When I told them about our
scheme, showed them the map of all this
land that is to be foreclosed, and how the

whole thing can be watered by a central
ditch, and all — you remember how it is out
there—one old rooster who has n't been out
of his own barn-yard in all his life, he up
and said, 'Yes, all very good, very good,
indeed, but supposing there is an Indian
outbreak — then where 's all our money for
your improvements gone?' Say, Jim, I just
fell right over dead. I met old man Wilson
there,—say, hold on here, what 's this I
hear? Is that right? Say, when 's it going
to be? There goes Martin and his kids,
taking them to Ali Baba; see what you 're
coming to. So you finally got your nerve
with you, did you? Go-o-od!''

With this outburst the bubbles of the pro-
moter's enthusiasm subsided. His companion reddened slightly at the raillery and
put one side of his under lip over his stubby
moustache in an embarrassed silence that
ended in a smirk.

"Well, Harris," he responded addressing
the taller friend, "you 've guessed it the
first time, I suppose. But we must all set-
tle down sooner or later, and anyway a man

do n't find that kind of a girl every day in the year." He paused a moment and Harris broke in—

"Oh, yes, if it comes to that, I suppose he must. I ain't a-kicking any, am I? Now, Jimmy, that 's a good boy, come and tell ownest own all about—" He was interrupted in his mock coddling by one of the drifters—who had been knocked from half a dozen groups, and had floated around in front of the formidable chairs. He was a portly old man, who had been a country banker in his day, and had come up and put new life into a wobbling institution after a local panic. He cut in with, "Well, what are you kids gassing about? Hello, there, Harris, did you make your irrigation scheme go?"

Harris looked up with annoyance written unmistakably on his face as he said, hardly civilly, "Yep," and lapsed into silence.

"Have any trouble getting at old Sage with my letter?" persisted the elder man.

"Nope," responded the younger. "Found him the only white man in New York. He

knew that there have n't been any grasshoppers in Kansas for twenty-five years. Only
man in town that did, though.''

There was a pause, in which Jim addressed
a remark to Harris about the big crowd that
was going to the theatre. A cable train had
just unloaded at the corner. The Kansas
man took the remark as general, and replied:

''Say, ain't they though; been that way,
too, every night this week.''

''Lookie quick!'' exclaimed Harris to his
companion. ''No — this side — there goes
Cameron; who 's that with her? Got a new
'mash'?''

''Why, you do n't mean to say that you
have n't heard,'' replied Jim, as he shifted
his position in his chair. ''She 's going to
get married, too. All the old birds going
home to nest.''

''Why, do you boys know Mrs. Cameron?'' asked the banker with some surprise. ''I did n't know she was in your set.''

''Ho! Ho! and so you know the widow,
too? L. No. 384 of the Cameron series,
eh, Jimmy?'' said Harris.

The woman, holding to a rather slender young fellow, perhaps thirty-five years old, dark and serious, who was watchfully bending over her, to catch her chatter, passed the club window, and disappeared in the cover of darkness that surrounded the arc light. She was a woman who, even on close inspection, showed little age, though instinct would have told a man — where a dozen other things would have told a woman — that she was thirty-three or thirty-four years old. As she scurried under the light, she seemed to cling to the man's figure, and tripped, rather than walked, along. One would have said that she was very happy as she passed, or that she could simulate happiness excellently.

"Me? Oh yes, I knew Mrs. Cameron when she was a little girl," said the elder man. "She came from my town — down in Baxter. Say, how is she making it here? I have n't seen her for going on two years now — two years next December, I think," mused the banker. The two young fellows looked quizzically at the old man, and then at each other. Then Harris shook his head and the short, fat, little man nodded back. They were satisfied that the old man was telling the truth.

"Well," began Jimmy, "she was n't cut out for a vagabond, and she has n't been making it very well, I guess."

"What 's the matter?" said the old man, who did not grasp the young fellow's meaning.

"Well, Mr. Martin, if you care to know, it 's nothing more unusual than wolves," replied Harris, as he swung his feet over the arm of the chair; "just plain, old-fashioned wolves. But I 'm mighty glad she is going to break for shelter. I 'm mighty glad—for her," Harris added in broken sentences. "Who 's the fellow, Jimmy?" he asked a moment later. By that time the slow processes of the elder man's mind had caught the idea that the woman under discussion was to be married, and he broke in without giving the young man a chance to answer his friend's question.

"Well, well, well, so Mrs. Cameron is

going to get married again! Her of all women!''

"Byers,"put in Jimmy in answer to Harris's question, as Martin rubbed his chin, and pulled up a chair to sit down and get the idea firmly fixed in his mind.

"Going to get married!" continued the old banker, thinking aloud. "Well, if that do n't beat all! Why, boys, I 've knowed her since she was a little slip of a girl — could n't a been more 'n ten years old — when they moved to Baxter. I see her graduate at the high school — handed her the diplomy, as president of the board, myself. And she 's going to get married again. Well, that gets me. I went to her wedding with old Cameron. She was the oldest of seven children, four of 'em girls, and Mrs. Griggs was mighty glad to get Mattie off her hands, though she was n't more'n eighteen when she was married; but every one thought she done so well, getting old Cameron, and his fine house that he 'd built her — and all. But I 'd 'a' thought she 'd 'a' got enough of marrying when she got done

with old Cameron. If ever a woman lived
ten years in hell, that woman did. And such
a nice, little woman, too. Seemed like she
tried ever so hard to make it pleasant; done
all her own work, flaxed around and fixed
up the house, putting little odds and ends
here and there, keeping up with the Chautau-
quy, and having the young folks around
her, and being just the world and all to
them babies of her'n. Used to hear her
singing at her work summer mornings before
I got up. (We lived next door neighbors.)
She used to know all the sick old ladies in
town, and take 'em jell and preserves and
elderberry wine, and go around and tell
everybody to run in and see 'em, before any-
one else in town had any idee they was sick.
She was that way, clean to the last, and
hardly anybody knowed they was anything
wrong, until she filed her suit. And we
did n't know it, ourselves, living right there,
until two years before, when old Cameron
come home and chased her out of the house,
one cold winter night, and she had to come
over to our house or freeze. Many and

many's the time she's stayed out all night
of summers, when he'd come home full and
ugly, rather than let the neighbors know.
Well, I must tell mother she's a-going to
get married again.''

The old man sat thinking silently, and
the two younger men evidently did not care
to speak. Each was wondering if the other
had not heard that story before, and each
was thinking hard things of the other, if he
had. Harris remembered the picture of a
petite figure in a red silk wrapper, sitting before the fire in a flat, popping corn, and
looking around to say in a soft voice, while
the fire-light made her face radiant: ''Tom,
I used to wear this wrapper, hundreds of
years ago, when I popped corn for my own
little girls.'' Something tightened in his
throat then, and there were tears in his
eyes when he had replied that evening.
So when the story came up again, he only
beat his stick on his shoe-tip and said
nothing. It was Martin who broke the
silence. He resumed where he had run
out of words.

"Old man Cameron, he war n't so mean
with men, that way. Take him in the bank,
and though he was in the opposition con-
cern, I can say that I never heard a man say
an unkind thing of him, and that 's a good
deal for a banker. My wife says Mrs. Cameron told her that there was times when
he would be awful sorry, and promise to do
better, and be as rational as you or me.
But he got them jealous spells and was a
regular devil, she said. Used to beat her, I
guess, though she never said so. One time,
— so she told my wife — after one of his tan-
trums — that was pretty near the end — he
had went down to Cincinnati, and while he
was gone, she made up her mind to leave
him. When he came home, he wanted to
be sugar and spice, and he seemed so peni-
tent. She had n't been more than civil to
him, for a year before, and the bad streak he
took made her see things could n't go on
that way. Well, sir, when he was down to
Cincinnati he turned in and bought her a
seal-skin sacque, and a new set of solid silver
knives and forks and spoons, and any

amount of little trinkets to wear. It was
the first time he had ever done anything of
the kind, and when she was getting supper
for him, she told my wife, he set the table
with the new things, and put the trinkets at
her place, and the sacque in her chair, and
then called her to see it. She come in and
shook her head, and turned to the kitchen-
door without a word. And she told my
wife if she 'd 'a' tried to said a word, she
would 'a' burst out crying.

"It was hard for her, but she did what
was for the best, I guess. 'T would n't 'a'
been six months before old man Cameron
would 'a' been up to his old tricks again.
She knew that then, just as well as I know
it now. But he was so big and strong, and
I suppose he was tender, too, when he felt
like it. But that was a mighty brave thing
to do, and I should n't wonder if she cried
that night, for the first time in years —
he 'd hardened her that way, you know,
for so long before."

There was no one with a voice to speak,
when the old man paused, so he sighed and

continued, "And now she's going to get married, eh? Who's the fellow?"

Morrison was the first to speak: "A man named Byers, of Denver," he said. "Did you know her after she came down here, Mr. Martin?"

"Only a little; she was trying to learn to be a trained nurse or something; used to see her at the theatre, with young fellows from the club. She come back to Baxter, now and then. Wife saw her there, and said she appeared to be cheerful. All the old ladies were tickled to death to see her. Made up a tea-party for her, about six months ago, when my wife and she happened to be back together at the same time, and my wife said they, every one of them old people—made over her like she was their own child, and she did seem to be so happy and all — to be back with 'em. And so you fellows say she tried to be a vagabond down here — poor little woman! And her just yearning for a home and some one to do for, all the time! What about the wolves, Harris? Tell me," said the elder man as he lighted a cigar and looked grimly at the charred match before throwing it away.

"There is n't much to tell, I guess. If every man would only tell what he knows, himself, there would be blame little. But as every man tells what he thinks a lot of other fellows know — it 's the old story, and a good deal too long. The chief trouble with wolves, you know, is their noise."

"It occurs to me, Harris," said young Jimmy Morrison with a knowing look sideways, "that you are getting mighty high-minded all of a sudden. I say it 's a shame about young Byers, of Denver. He seems to be a pretty decent fellow."

"Has a little money, has n't he?" chipped in Harris.

"Sheep-buyer for a packing house, I believe. We had some dealing with him," said the banker, as he puffed, and put his hands back of his head as a pillow for a moment.

"Something like that," said Jimmy. "Anyway, he looks like an honest fellow.

Somebody ought to tell him about Cameron. It 's tough to see him going into this thing — like an ox to the slaughter.'' The speaker evidently thought he had said something funny, for he laughed a dry, mean, little laugh. It may have irritated Harris, for he turned on the younger man quickly and said:

"Oh, you do, do you? Well, Jimmy Morrison, maybe you would like to have the same man, who tells what he has heard of this woman, tell the same thing to the future Mrs. Morrison, a few weeks before the cards are out.'' He, too, laughed derisively, and as he sat looking at his smirking companion, who was clearly proud rather than ashamed at the thrust, Martin arose, evidently aroused from a reverie. It was in a soft, deep voice, a trifle husky — such as old men not used to scenes use on occasions — that he replied:

''Do you boys know you are talking of a human being? This business that is so funny to you, it is all of that woman's life! It 's your farce, maybe; but, great God, it 's her— her — her tragedy!''

After an abashed silence Martin walked slowly away from the two friends. Each one thought, for an instant, of a face that he remembered, lighted up by the warm glow of the grate fire. Each knew the story as the old man had told it. Each thought of the way he had heard it. It was fully a minute after the old man walked away with his hands behind him, when Harris spoke:

"Funny thing, this life, ain't it?" he said.

"Yes, damned funny—the more you know of it," said Morrison as he arose. "Isn't it getting about 'that time?' Whose turn is it to buy the old Falernian?"

The Reading of the Riddle

"Dear, was it really you and I?
In truth the riddle's ill to read,
So many are the deaths we die
Before we can be dead indeed."
—*W. E. Henley.*

THE town of Willow Creek lies at the junction of a rivulet of that name, with the Big Muddy. But the people of that community being born scoffers, have changed the name of the Big Muddy in common parlance to "Mud Crick," and, transformed by the alchemy of popular depreciation, the name of the town itself has shriveled into "Willer Crick." It might have been something of a town, as towns go in the West, but instead of pulling with his neighbors for the success of the town, each of its founders spent his time making fun of the pretensions of others. When there was talk on the part of "old man" Mead, the prime-

val postmaster, of securing the government
land office for Willow Creek, the Indian
trader, and the saloon keeper, and the black-
smith, made great sport of the old man's
ambition.   A few years later, when civiliza-
tion had crowded in with a hotel, a lumber
yard, a new saloon, and a barber shop, some
one spoke of starting a newspaper; but the
laugh that went up from Willow Creek was
the only unanimity that greeted Editor Mc-
Cray when his back was turned.   But the
newspaper came, and so did the people, and
they kept coming, until, when the ''boom ''
of the later eighties struck Kansas, it found
Willow Creek with about two thousand
scoffing inhabitants.   The effect of the
''boom '' on the town was strange indeed.
It was a contagious mental disease, and
when it attacked the two thousand suf-
ferers from chronic melancholia, its effect
was like the confusion of tongues.   Every
man had his own scheme for the salvation
of Willow Creek, and every other man
jeered at him.   One man wanted to start a
woolen mill on ''Mud Crick,'' and after the

walls were up and the machinery in, Willow Creek split its sides with laughter, when the enterprising man found there was no wool in Lincoln county. An enthusiastic man, who bored and struck salt, was the town joke, when he discovered that the railroad rates were so high, that he could not evaporate and ship the salt at a profit. An iron foundry, a deserted college, a clock factory, and a flour mill to-day stand as monuments to the energy of the "boom," and the potent influence of the organized scoffers.

But, in one way or another, the "boom" seemed to bring wealth to Willow Creek. And with wealth, came some attempts at the organization of polite society. There were innumerable young real estate agents, young doctors, young lawyers, and clerks, all from the East, in the village; and these, with the daughters of the early settlers and such friends as they chanced to make in the high school, constituted the aristocracy of the town. It was a vulnerable aristocracy, and the scoffers made sad havoc with it. Fathers, who had carried their sweethearts—

now their wives—across the Big Muddy on their backs to and from the dances at Jack Armstrong's ranch, were too common, and too voluble in Willow Creek, to permit the daughters and sons of the town to assume very much dignity. If a family put on many airs, the members of a dozen families in town would tell newcomers how the would-be fashionables had received "aid" from the committee, in the grasshopper year.

It was said of Flora McCray, who went to boarding school and came back, timid, retiring, and distinctly unsocial, that, "She need n't hold herself so high. If her father would only pay back the money he stole in the school land fraud she would be as common as anybody." But the girl paid no heed to these rumors, if she heard them. She quietly filled her small sphere, bounded on one side by her meek-voiced mother and her busy father, on another side by her church and her "church social," on a third side by a very brief glimpse of a very big world and her memory of it, and on the fourth side by occasional day dreams and night thoughts, pretty much the same as those which come to any young girl of good health, good spirits, and twenty-one years, who has never had a sweetheart.

After the "boom" had passed, Willow Creek saw the dress suits that had many and many a time danced to the sound of revelry by night in the opera house flit away. Flora McCray probably knew nothing of the appearance, nor of the departure of these formal trappings. They seldom appeared at the church socials, and when they were gone from the gatherings of politer society, the young woman did not miss them in her humble walk. She had never attended a dance; not that she was too strong in her piety to have gone, but because no one had ever thought of asking her. Dancing, during the days of the "boom" was the chief, if not the only social diversion, in what was known as the best society of the place. So it was said that the McCray girl "never went out."

As the reaction, caused by the decadence of real estate prices set in, Willow Creek became poorer. As the young men, who paid for the orchestras, and halls, and flowers, gradually left town, the young women, who formerly frequented receptions, parties, and balls, were seen more and more often at the "church socials." After a two-years ineffectual struggle Willow Creek gave it up; the town could no longer support two branches of society, and the "church crowd" and the "dance crowd" merged into one. The union was a very sensible one, yet every one laughed at it and said that the church people were getting giddy, or that "the aristocracy had made a fine 'come down' from its high horse." Of a bevy of girls who gave broom-brigade drills and milk-maid conventions, and who conducted "toe socials," for the benefit of the library or the temperance society, Flora McCray made one. But it was merely a numerical one. As a leader, a planner, and a schemer, she was less than an integer.

She had no intimates, and unless a crowd was present, or numbers were needed, no one thought of her. She went everywhere with her parents. Young men were scarce, and other girls, more designing than she, never thought of wasting masculine material on her.

When it was announced that the entire social body of Willow Creek was going out to Robinson's for a "taffy pull," one Saturday night, the rest of Willow Creek laughed. The town people sneered at the young women who had planned the party, and intimated that the night ride out to Robinson's and back was an heroic measure; and they laughed at old man Robinson and his family for tolerating people who would snub them if they came to town, and lastly they laughed at the young men who would have to pay the livery bills.

Saturday morning, John Howard, Mr. McCray's partner in the stock business, came up from the farm on Dry Creek, and after going over some details of business, McCray asked his partner to Sunday dinner, as was his custom, when the young man was in town, and the invitation was accepted. During the "boom" Howard had made money. He had mingled with what is known as the "swell set" of Willow Creek, and though not a favorite at the flood of the "boom," the very fact that he had the social instinct, made him a necessity in society at its ebb.

Soon after leaving his partner's office, he had learned of the plans for the "taffy pull," that evening. He was urged to go, and finding that all the "rigs" were full, and that all the girls of his "set" were provided with escorts, in a moment of despairing inspiration the young man sent a note to his partner's daughter, asking for "the pleasure of her company." His invitation was accepted, and late that afternoon, Flora McCray stepped into a buggy with the first beau she had ever had, and headed a long procession for Robinson's.

*   *   *   *   *   *   *   *

Some one had stopped the clock that night, and the young women, putting on their wraps, guessed that it was nearly midnight, when the "taffy pull" at Robinson's broke up. As Flora McCray sat alone in the Robinson parlor waiting to hear the grinding of wheels across the gravelled path that would herald her escort's buggy, she went over the evening's impressions in her mind. She decided that it had been a very pleasant evening. She had never before found herself surrounded by the masterful attentions of a young man. She was pleased with his business-like devotion to her coffee-cup, and was amused, yet a little startled, when he piled a monument of cake upon her plate and called on every one to pass things down his way as Miss McCray was very hungry. It was a new sensation to find herself a part of the merriment. Heretofore, she had been only a spectator at such scenes. And now that it was all over, she felt herself still a spectator, and in the mood of a spectator, she smiled deprecatingly as she thought of the courteous attentions of her father's friend. And thus, with a mind isolated from the vain world by such reflections, she started with Howard on their homeward ride.

It was a blustering, cloudy night. The

freakish wind scurried across fields, pirou-
etted around corners, scampered through
hedges, and impishly pulled the dry, scrag-
gly grass of the roadside, till the bald, old
earth winced and shivered with pain. Howard was the last to leave, and as he got into
the buggy, after closing the last gate, the
rollicking wind tugged viciously at a corner of the lap-robe, like a playful puppy.
The girl shivered as Howard leaned over to
tuck the robe more snugly around her. She
slipped gently from her attitude of passive
placidity to one of unconscious, yet active
interest, in what appeared to be the strange,
new face her companion seemed to wear in
the darkness.   At first they chatted on
about the commonplaces of Willow Creek.
Flora McCray tried again and again to asso-
ciate her recollection of the familiar face of
her father's partner with the smooth-shaven
face so near her in the night.   Her repeated
efforts were tantalizing.   Little by little,
did the wizard of the night weave her fancies, and then herself into the woof of his
uncanny spell.   Not only was she with a

stranger, but she was herself a stranger to herself. Nor was the spirit of the dark contented till he had sold the man, also, into the slavery of the shadow world. Then the grim old wizard beckoned the wind with a hand of cloud, and bade it plash little gusts of mist into the two unreal, spell-bound faces. It may have been the cold. It may have been the utter lonesomeness of the night that drew her close to him, but she came, and was not afraid.

Again he reached over her, and again tucked the wraps closer than ever about her, and the fumbling touches of his hands awakened the girl's new self to a delightful realization of the fact that a new being had come to her out of the darkness. She came even closer to this new-found presence, and almost cuddled against the man's great coat, and snuggled under his arm, that rested loosely upon the cushions behind her. Their talk, which had been growing more and more serious, gradually stopped. The horses jogged on in the night, and the rattle of the harness and the wheels beat a broken tattoo, muffled at times by the complaining wind, while the wizard of the dark worked his grotesque enchantment.

"Are you cold — dear?" the young man asked, when he felt her come close to him. His words and his tone startled the girl and almost broke the spell. Flora McCray struggled a moment with the Girl in the Dark, and shuddered in despair as a voice from the Girl, who felt a strong arm quiet her, answered: "A little."

Scoff your noisy guffaws with the flapping curtains, whistle your sneers in the dead weed stalks, and mumble your pious warnings among the telegraph wires by the roadside, wind of the Willow Creek prairies; you cannot break the spell. Throw yourself upon the hill-side, roll over and over in your convulsions of derision. The charm you would dissolve is only sweetened, when the sorcerer of the night turns your antics into uncouth mysteries, and your cachinations into worldless passion songs.

* * * * *

As the lights of the town came in sight

the young couple grew silent. A turn in the road brought the buggy under the white glare of an electric light. Flora McCray was sitting upright with her hands folded under the robe, and Howard, with the whip and the lines in his hands, was consciously clucking at the horses. Each saw the other's face clearly, and as they crossed the circle of light the man spoke:

"It must be two o'clock."

The girl did not reply, and the young man leaned over to look out of the buggy, as if to scan the clouds. The prospect did not altogether satisfy him and he said:

"It's going to be a pretty gloomy Sunday, I guess."

As Howard put out his arms to help her from the buggy she barely touched his outstretched hand, and her decided shyness surprised him. In a bewilderment of confusion he said:

"You have made me very happy to-night — Miss McCray. Shall I speak to your father when I come out to dinner to-morrow?"

The girl did not reply, but went up the steps and into the house, while the young man climbed into his buggy, and beat time with the whip to the tune he was whistling, as he gave the horses the rein for the stable.

Flora McCray locked the door and slipped the bolt as quietly as she could. She blew out the light in the parlor and stole noiselessly upstairs, avoiding, as was her wont in using the stairs at night, the creaky step at the landing, that always wakened her mother. After entering her room she turned up the light and at once began taking off her outer wraps. This prim, shy, old-fashioned girl had, from her earliest childhood, observed habits of precise neatness. This evening, she went about her room, hanging up every garment that belonged on a hook, and folding away every one that belonged elsewhere. To outward view, she was a placid, methodical, emotionless being — perhaps she, herself, did not notice that she avoided facing the mirror as she took down her hair — yet strong feelings were working within her. Just before going to bed she started to put

away her hat.   She picked it up.   The velvet and the ribbon seemed crushed.   She
put out her hand to smooth them.   A hot
flush of recollection swept over her, and she
put the hat down.   She did not look at it
again, but blew out the light and went to
bed with her face turned from the guilty re-
minder.   And all night long Flora McCray
lashed herself for the folly of the Girl in the
Dark.   And all night long Flora McCray
scourged her very self for a very impossible
self, blaming her very modest self for an
hour that she could not explain, and putting
her flushed face under the pillow when she
remembered for what it had been upturned
so eagerly in the dark.   In her abject remorse, it seemed to her that she was the only
guilty one — the man was only a means, not
an agent in the fancied transgression.   As
she remembered it, she had made all the ad-
vances; he had only been kind and good to
her.

The next morning, all of Willow Creek
knew that John Howard had taken Flora
McCray to Robinson's the night before, and

that he was going to eat Sunday dinner with the McCrays that afternoon. But the town, as usual, was divided. One half claimed that the McCrays had to have all of Howard's money, or they would fail; and the other half held that John Howard was going to marry Flora McCray to keep the old man from prosecuting him for running off mortgaged cattle and reporting them as dead. And in the whole town no one could have been so thoroughly surprised as was Mr. McCray, when his daughter said to him, "Father, if Mr. Howard says anything to you about me, you will tell him — that — I cannot — marry him."

McCray and his daughter were walking along the narrow, rough sidewalk toward the church, when these words were spoken. The mother had dropped back, and was not in hearing distance. McCray could only find voice for a few exclamatory "whys" and "whats" before his daughter had said firmly, "You will be sure, won't you, Father?" and was waiting for her mother to catch up with them. After the service, the women, Flora and her mother among them, hurried home to attend to the feast of the day, and the men, after lounging around the postoffice, sauntered home, newspapers in hand. With this crowd, came McCray and his young partner. For a while in their walk they talked very low and earnestly, and then seemed to cheer up and be concerned only with the commonplaces.

At the dinner table the young people met for the first time that day. Flora McCray felt keenly, and with a twinge of anguish, that the young man's cordial suavity in greeting her was only inspired by gratitude for her generosity in releasing him from any obligation.

She met his eye, and thought she read there a recollection of everything that had been. Then, as she looked down and away, all the sweetness and unreality of the night's ride was made real to her. A turn of his head brought his profile into relief, and she thought of how handsome he had looked out in the night, and of how tender he had been with her. While the young man chatted on idly with her father, the girl was silent, as she always was, when there were visitors at the house.

After dinner the men went into the parlor, where they smoked and talked alone, while the women put away the best china, afraid to trust it to the "hired girl." Finally, young Howard and Mr. McCray thought that the evening mail would be in and distributed. They put on their overcoats and were in the hall, when the elder man opened the dining-room door and said:

"Mother, John thinks it's time to go, and I am going to walk down to the post-office with him."

When the front door closed Mrs. McCray said:

"What a nice, young man John Howard is, isn't he?"

"Oh, yes, he is nice enough, I guess," answered the daughter, rising to go to her room.

As she neared the top of the stairs, Flora McCray quickened her pace. She ran through the upper hall. Once in her room, she went straight to the dresser, where the rumpled hat was still lying. The lonely girl stood before it a moment, and then, stooping awkwardly, touched the crumpled velvet with pursed, uncertain lips, as one ashamed. It may have been the dusk in the room, or it may have been the ghost of an odor from a cigar, that transported this unschooled heart back to the darkness, and the joy of a first caress. But dusk, or ghost, or something, came to this shy girl there, and nerved her whole being, so that she was no longer awkward, no longer uncertain, nor in any wise ashamed. The pretty velvet toy she made her shrine, and in her worship she kissed it, rubbed it with her burning cheek, and buried her face in its sacred folds.

In Willow Creek where they scoff and higgle over sordid things, in Willow Creek the hard, the arid, the barren, they say — no matter what — but in and out of the narrow ways, turning the sharp corners with the rest, with tired feet, and timid, unsure hands, there goes a woman whose womanhood came to her as a dream — in the night.

The Chief Clerk's Christmas

HAWKINS, the chief clerk, was a grim man. He had little to say; he did not even patronize the elevator boy, and he never talked with the office girls about his necktie. He did not speak at all, except to give orders to the clerks, who bent over their desks with conspicuous industry, when he was around, and gossiped about him when he was gone. It was admitted by them all that he was smart; there was a suspicion among the younger men that he was wicked, and among the girls, who nagged at the typewriters, there was a hope that he was both; so they talked about his meek-voiced stenographer, and said that Hawkins was a beast. The former chief clerk had been very gay, and had danced around the office singing the refrain of topical songs, pretending to look over the clerks' shoulders to

see what they were about.   But Hawkins
stayed in his office and pressed buttons.
His industry was proverbial all over the
building, and the janitor and the office boy
had a song about it, that they sang down in
the basement to the tune of a darkey
break-down, "Sho'tnun Braid."   It ran:

> "What's Hawkins do-un'?
> Sittun at 'is desk.
> What's Hawkins do-un'?
> Gawd knows best."

Neither the janitor nor the office boy was
a poet, but the recitative voiced a popular
inquiry, and within a week after it was
evolved, it was everybody's property. Once,
in the summer, Hawkins was not in his
room.   He was absent three days, and all in
the building wondered.   He came back and
said nothing; but the general auditor told
his chief clerk, who told a subordinate, who
flew with the news into Hawkins's depart-
ment, that the chief clerk of the freight and
traffic manager had been home to attend his
mother's funeral. The men tried to show him
that they were sorry for him, and the girls

watched him more closely than ever to see how he was "taking it." Consequently, they still thought him a beast. The office boy saw a photograph of a little old woman in a cap, under a row of pigeon holes on his desk, and before night every one in the office had made a trip to see what she looked like. The women thought he did n't take after her a bit, and the men, having satisfied their curiosity, had no opinion at all.

Nobody knew anything about Hawkins before he came to the chief clerk's desk. The under clerks could never have found out the facts about him, which are that he once lived in a little country town, called Willow Creek, and that his father was as grim as he, and had died when Hawkins was young. Hawkins and his mother and elder sister had lived together; Hawkins, taciturn and sullen; his mother as tender as he would allow; and his sister petulant, but patient — in the long run. He had left home, barely grunting good-bye to the household, and his mother made her home with his sister, who soon married. He went home

each Christmas, at first, on business; then
because his mother, who wrote to him with
religious regularity, had begged him to
come, and finally, as he grew older and
came to know himself and the people better,
because he liked to go.   One Christmas
night he unbosomed himself to his mother;
told her his plans and all that he hoped to
be and to do, and the tears came to her
eyes.   He kissed her when he left that time
and wrote long letters to her.   She was his
only confidant.   He said much in the letters
that he would not have spoken for worlds.
God only knows how desolate he was when
she died.

As Christmas time drew near, Hawkins
was habitually planning to go home, and
then suddenly remembering — and wondering what he would do.   People who said
he was a firm man and never changed his
decision should have seen his heart as the
holidays approached.   To-day he was decided to go; on the morrow he was trying
to find excuses for staying in town.   One
day, as he was sitting at his desk, gazing va-

cantly for a moment at the photograph, his stenographer saw his face flush; that evening he told the general manager he would be off Christmas, and Hawkins was a man who thought twice, but spoke once. He had decided to do something.

He took Christmas dinner with his sister and her family in Willow Creek, and they tried to turn the subject to his mother, but he cut them, and closed up like a shell. After dinner he said he was going for a walk. The sister's husband politely offered to go with him, but it was plain that Hawkins wished to be alone.

It was a clear day—almost like spring. The ground was soft, and tufts of blue grass came up between the stones of the sidewalks and touched his feet. He walked to the village greenhouse, and succeeded in buying some flowers. He did it as though he always bought flowers Christmas day. Then he struck up the country road towards the cemetery. His face was hard and sour. He felt that the people were looking at him, and the hatred of their curiosity all but

showed itself in his features, as he glared at
the questioning sexton, who unlocked the
iron gate. He walked rapidly through, and
did not look back.

When he reached his mother's tomb, he
stopped and gazed anxiously in every direction. Seeing no one, he took off the wrap-
pings and placed the flowers awkwardly on
the grave. It was a strange, unsatisfy-
ing thing to do, and he wondered why he
had felt an uncontrollable desire to do it.
It was the first tender thing he had ever
planned and executed, and as its accomplishment brought only disappointment, it
made him feel lonelier than ever in the
world. He sat down on the seamy, new-
laid patches of grass-sod over the grave, and
bit the skin of his upper lip; he saw the
sexton approaching, and rose suddenly.
Hawkins tried to avoid the old man, but he
could not. The sexton asked if everything
was all right, and was just launching out
into sympathetic condolence, when Hawkins
handed him a bill, saying, ''Is this enough?''
and turned and left him.

He was at his desk the next day, and from the further end of the hall his tittering clerks heard the office boy call to the janitor who was polishing the banister on the next floor:

> "What's Hawkins do-un',
> Settun at 'is desk?"

And the janitor answered:

> "What's Hawkins do-un'?
> Gawd knows best."

The Story of a Grave

THERE is a place in the Great American Desert where green grass grows. At the head of an estuary of the great dry sea, where a long arm of white alkali runs up among the foothills of the mountains, stands an inviting tavern. It is upon the hillside. Just below it, the garden hose and the landscape gardener, with water carried in troughs from the mountains, have wrought a miracle of green. Trees, blue-grass, flowers, wax strong and beautiful in the artificial oasis. Children and young men and maidens romp on the verdant mat, spread at the point of the estuary, and upon the hillside a score of languid guests sit in the healing sun, and look down upon the picture, and out into the endless miles of white sand that stretch billowy and fantastic into the blue of the horizon.

Most of these idlers on the broad piazza of the tavern are invalids.   It is a place of invalids.   Here hundreds of wretched bodies are dragged by a tragic love of life.   Here scores of souls watch other souls flicker and die out, and still hope on and wait, while the oil of life burns smudgy and low.   There are those whom the sunshine and the dry clear air win back to life.   But the dead are there.   On the broad veranda — a very citadel of life — the dead are embattled, fighting with time.   It is a most hideous battle, and all so hushed and sepulchral are its manœuvres, that Life takes no heed of the empty pageant.

Armed in such a combat sat Hawkins, the chief clerk, a grim man, dark, pallid, sinister. Of what, out in the world of life, Hawkins had been chief clerk, it does not matter now. He had been a busy man, firm, taciturn, self-contained, repellent.   He sat now at his post in the battle, sneering at the folly of those about him who were trying to wrest a few mortal moments from eternity.   It did not occur to him that he was one of the soldiers in the fight, yet by them he was classed among the hopeless.

For a long time, as days go, Hawkins had been sitting in this sentry box, when his captain — the doctor — ordered him into the infantry, and told him to march for dear life. Hawkins left the guards upon the terrace with loathing. He had a gnawing contempt for their silly belief, that they were warding off the enemy; that they were conquering death; and as the grim man set out upon his daily walk down the hill, and around the beach of the great, shimmering, dead sea of sand and dust, he speculated diabolically on which of the enthusiasts would be in the hospital when he should return. During the first week of his marching orders, he made exactly the same journey every day. He noticed everything along his path. He was interested in nothing. In his mind the objects he saw were catalogued, but never referred to by his memory. There was a huge bluff, a railroad bridge, a quarry, a barbed wire fence, enclosing a grave, a mud house, a herder, some sheep, a steep hill, a

water trough, a cross road, and a pine grove,
on the hill over which he came back to his
starting point. None of these objects was
dignified by a prominence in his mind. One
day, attracted by the most unimportant
detail in the landscape, Hawkins started to
walk a few rods from his path, that he might
examine more closely the grave, fenced in
with barbed wire to keep the ghoulish desert
beasts away. A second thought made the
digression from the path the line of an
ellipse, and he followed his course without
veering.

There were days when Hawkins spoke to
none of the hotel guests, and the lack of
interest in the place weighed heavily upon
him. As he sat for hours after his walks,
gazing between the hills that penned out
the desert, the spot where the grave dotted
the surface of the plain kept drawing his
eyes to it, in an annoying manner. He tried
turning his back to the spot, but in his
fancy the dot appeared on the picture of
the scene, and he grew black with anger.
Then he went to his room and forgot all

about it until the next day on his walk, or after it.

As he took his lonely walk at the end of that fortnight, the grave began to irritate him. It aroused a certain curiosity within him, which was very distasteful. It was his pride that nothing outside of himself and his personal environment, interested him. The mound in some way pushed through his armour of selfishness, and he was pricked with what seemed a senseless desire to see it close at hand. He fought the whim, but a dozen times he was compelled to turn back in his path, so strongly did he seem drawn to the spot. There was nothing else to occupy his mind and one night, after his return from a walk, raging at his folly, the grave began to haunt his wakeful night-fancies. The next afternoon he walked over to the enclosure, thinking that he would be no longer disturbed by the thing if he examined it closely.

Hawkins saw only an adult's grave with a cactus upon it. At the head was a wooden board. At the foot was a broad peg. The barbed wire was torn away at one end — perhaps by some stray animal, wandering in the night. Hawkins did not approach nearer than a rod from the fence, and he turned quickly as though he had overcome his weakness, when he had gathered these details in his mind.

The next day he came closer, and the day following, after a night in which he was kept awake, frenzied because of a gnawing ache to pick the cactus root out of the dead man's side, Hawkins came to the fence and leaned upon the post, looking back toward the hotel to see if the group on the veranda could see him. He did not touch the cactus, and not until he had straightened up to go did he so much as glance at the mound. He read the name on the headboard — and hurried away with fear dogging his steps. He looked behind by sheer force of will. It was the one name in the world that Hawkins loved to hate. With it came the recollection of the woman whom the grim man was proud that he had forgotten.

At the road around the hill he checked

his nervous gait and walked slowly back to the hotel. But all the way up the hillside the headboard kept rising before him with the word "Zain" over the word "Thweke."

Hawkins sat in his chair on the veranda when he had returned, and looked over the white plain, glistening in the sun. The blot on the white floor in the distance seemed magnified in his eyes. He fancied he could distinguish the headboard from the fence. Then he began to fight with the spell. He reasoned that it was an accident, and it came over him with a chill, that he had been drawn to the place by an irresistible force. At this conclusion he smiled sardonically and lighted a cigar.

He believed he had conquered the hallucination by giving it full rein. Then he began to hate his old enemy. Hawkins had not known that the man was dead until that day. He mused pleasurably upon the cactus. The doctor, seeing Hawkins in the sunset air with a cigar, swore at him, and the grim man went in doors. He was proud to be alive.   His pride amounted almost to a thrill.

Hawkins went to sleep early that night. When the lights in the hotel were extinguished he wakened from a dream about figures and business, and felt that there was something important on his mind. Then he remembered the discovery on the headboard. He trailed over his treasure with the harrow of his hate. There seemed to him to be a certain compensation in it, a kind of gruesome poetic justice. He wondered if there could be such a thing as that. If not, he asked himself, why had he been drawn to that lonely mound of sand and stones and desert weeds? What, except some force outside himself, he reasoned, had torn him away from his habits, and put that headboard before his eyes? The headboard seemed to be pictured in the shadows on the wall. What had brought him to it, he wondered? And then he dared not face an uncanny question that was all but forming itself in his mind. He tried to shake it off. He mentally smiled at himself for being afraid of the supernatural. He tried to think of something else; he began counting, finally it came. A sentence formed in his mind, "Was it the dead man's spirit?"

When he aroused himself his mouth was dry, and he was wet with perspiration. Hawkins' normal mind then took control of his fancy and his hate for the conquered foe burned fiercely. The woman kept coming into his malignant speculations. He wondered if she had taken the man's name. He was curious to know if she had come with his enemy into the desert where he died. Hawkins pictured them together on the terrace. Then his sick fancy painted them in the very room where he was lying. For a moment he was in mental hell. A footfall startled him. He sprang to the floor to ring the bell and to ascertain if his imaginings had any foundation in fact. When the boy came Hawkins asked for icewater, and upon getting it sipped it, as he stood looking out at the quiet stars and the moon, and listening to the sheep-bells, and to the dogs barking out on the floor of the desert, beyond the grave.   This soothed him, and he slept.

The day following that night, and for many days thereafter, Hawkins stood gazing at the ugly sand heap in its barbed wire prison, exulting in his heart at the dead man's desolation.   The moments he spent thus were almost happy ones for the grim man.   His fancy made morbid pictures; and the figures of the man and woman danced before his eyes in a thousand horrid day-dreams.   Once he kicked the headboard, and sneered at himself for so doing.   Then Hawkins saw how like a cur he was.

After that there were three in his circle of hate.

One day, loathing himself, he began to wonder what had ever induced the woman to promise to love and to honor him.   He re-called cowardly words he had spoken to her. Revelations of his own cruelty and meanness were made to him, and ghostly memories that he had strangled years before, came flitting back.   He remembered a white face looking up to him, and a thick voice begging him to be good to her; and then with a shuddering blush he recalled the jealous taunt, with which he had jeered a reply. He saved his most blighting maledictions for himself. A cancer of remorse began rotting his heart.   .

He was oppressed with a sense of having done a terrible wrong. The face of the woman whom he had forgotten, rose and floated on his stagnant fancies. Dialogues, that he had crowded into what seemed to him oblivion came trooping back, and whispered themselves into his ear. In each of these pictures and voices he saw his own selfishness. Hawkins began to know himself as he was known. A love that he had cursed and trampled out with his physical heel in a fit of rage, began to glow and warm his being. A faint blaze of sentiment fluttered in his heart, and one night, looking from his bed at the moon, Hawkins wondered where in the world it shone on her who was once his wife. Then he got up and pulled down the window curtain.

A miracle was wrought on the day that a

shriveled tear trembled in his eye. He
went to the grave, and stood a longer time
than usual after that. He left the place
with a sigh, and walked slowly with his
eyes upon the ground. He walked slowly,
partly from choice, partly because his
former gait sapped his strength. On the
veranda they were counting the weeks left
him.

He now went to the mound every day for
company. To those whom he met in the
routine of his physical life, Hawkins pre-
served his cold exterior. His habit of aus-
terity was not broken. Yet strange things
were working within his breast. He had
lived his life alone, and no one outside himself could know of the softening of his heart.
The visits to the grave grew necessary
to his happiness. For the first time in his
life, Hawkins felt as desolate as he really
was. He visited the grave, as a man of or-
dinary temperament would call upon a com-
rade. When his strength permitted a trip
every other day, only, he sat in his room
looking out between the hills at the plain,

and at the fascinating dot upon the white stretch of sand and alkali.

It was at these times that Hawkins began to try to recall the possible good qualities of his dead enemy. Hawkins remembered how he had condemned the man out of hand, when his name was first brought up, because Thweke wrote a copy-book hand. Hawkins remembered also, that, he had sneered at the man on account of a certain curl of the moustache; and that the fellow had incurred a husbandly hate, by knowing how to play the piano. Remembering these prejudices, Hawkins tried to make some entries on the other side of the account.

As the Shadow flitted nearer and nearer to the grim man, now confined to his barren room more closely than before, he began to lose the horror he once had felt at what he fancied might be the presence of the dead. One day he found himself curiously listening for some token from the dead man in the grave. His mood was not one of horror, but of longing. He reasoned that his strange finding of this grave, the inexplicable

power that drew him against his will and
against his nature to the lonely spot, and
the influence which it had wrought upon his
life indicated the presence of some outside
power. He built up a theory of hypnot-
ism from disembodied spirits, and sat watching for a signal to verify through his material senses, the existence of the supernatural
force, with which his spirit seemed to have
been communing. In this frame of mind he
forgot the wasting of the flesh. He sat by
his window, overlooking the desert, and
mused by the hour upon life and the coming
of the end. His whole being was softened
by the approaching dissolution of his body.

He longed for some sign that would tell
him that he had fellowship — real and palpable—with the spirit of the man in the deserted
grave. But the sign did not come. He
traced false signs to their natural causes,
and was sad. The habit of a lifetime, as a
scoffer, strangled credulity, even though it
was the child of hope. So Hawkins sat in
the silence, listening and waiting for the
greater silence.

There came a time when he rallied — when he left the window for the veranda. Then it was that a great yearning came to his heart to go and lie prone upon the grave and to be as simple as a child in grief. He could not explain this yearning; he did not try to analyze it. He felt some way that it was a thing the woman would have done, and the desire became a master passion. It seemed cold to him on the porch; but out on the desert the sun shone gaily and seductively. Day after day, he walked the length of the veranda. He seemed to be gaining strength. There was a day when he walked the entire distance around the hotel twice, without sitting or resting. It was a day of triumph. That night he planned his journey to the fence and the mound between the foothills.

His mental strain brought a slight relapse in his malady. He did not notice it the next morning. He kept his plans to himself. That afternoon he slipped away. Slowly, slowly, he crept down the terraces. He sat down often by the wayside. A notion that he was making a pilgrimage that she—Hawkins only thought of the woman as "she," now —would have him make, warmed something in his grim heart, not unlike a tenderness. He was very weak, and his emotions were loose. He took every tortured step as a penance, and his throat tightened with a boyish joy, as he thought he was doing something the woman would approve.

Once he fainted when he sat down by a stone. When he returned to consciousness he hurried on in a dazed, fumbling sort of way. He felt then that it would be his last visit to the grave, but he was not sad. He was only glad that he had come in Her name. Pride was purged from his flesh. His heart was that of a little child. He uttered foolish, little prayers that were bargains with God for strength to reach his goal. When he reached it, he crawled into the wire enclosure, weak and panting. There they found Hawkins at the close of day, grim, repellent of feature, apart from his kind, alone in his very death. Men said it was a fitting end for him.

The Home-coming of Colonel Hucks

A GENERATION ago, a wagon covered with white canvas turned to the right on the California road, and took a northerly course toward a prairie stream that nestled just under a long, low bluff. When the white pilgrim, jolting over the rough, unbroken ground, through the tall "blue stem" grass, reached a broad bend in the stream, it stopped. A man and a woman emerged from under the canvas, and stood for a moment facing the wild, green meadow, and the distant hills. The man was young, lithe, and graceful, but despite his boyish figure the woman felt his unconscious strength, as he put his arm about her waist. She was aglow with health; her fine, strong, intelligent eyes burned with hope, and her firm jaw was good to behold. They stood gazing at the virgin field a moment in silence. There were tears in the woman's eyes, as she looked up after the kiss and said:

"And this is the end of our wedding journey; and — and — the honey-moon — the only one we can ever have in all the world — is over."

The horses, moving uneasily in their sweaty harness, cut short the man's reply. When he returned, his wife was getting the cooking utensils from under the wagon, and life—stern, troublous—had begun for them.

It was thus that young Colonel William Hucks brought his wife to Kansas.

They were young, strong, hearty people, and they conquered the wilderness. A home sprang up in the elbow of the stream. In the fall, long rows of corn shocks trailed what had been the meadow. In the summer the field stood horse-high with corn. From the bluff, as the years flew by, the spectator might see the checker-board of the farm, clean cut, well kept, smiling in the sun. Little children frolicked in the king row, and hurried to school down the green

lines of the lanes where the hedges grow.
Once, a slow procession, headed by a spring
wagon with a little black box in it, might
have been seen filing between the rows of the
half-grown poplar trees and out across the
brown, stubble-covered prairie, to the desolate hill and the graveyard. Now, neighbors
from miles around may be heard coming in
rattling wagons across vale and plain, laden
with tin presents; after which the little home
is seen ablaze with lights, while the fiddle
vies with the mirth of the rollicking party,
dancing with the wanton echoes on the bluff
across the stream.

There were years when the light in the
kitchen burned far into the night, when two
heads bent over the table, figuring to make
ends meet. In these years the girlish figure
became bent, and the light faded in the woman's eyes, while the lithe figure of the man
was gnarled by the rigors of the struggle.
There were days — not years, thank God —
when lips forgot their tenderness; and, as
fate tugged fiercely at the curbed bit, there
were times, when souls rebelled, and cried

out in bitterness and despair, at the rough-
ness of the path.

In this wise went Colonel William Hucks
and his wife through youth into maturity,
and in this wise they faced towards the
sunset.

He was tall, with a stoop; grizzled,
brawny, perhaps uncouth in mien. She was
stout, unshapely, rugged; yet her face was
kind and motherly. There was a boyish
twinkle left in her husband's eyes, and a
quaint, quizzing, one-sided smile often
stumbled across his care-furrowed counte-
nance. As the years passed, Mrs. Hucks
noticed that her husband's foot fell heavily
when he walked by her side, and the pang
she felt when she first observed his plodding
step was too deep for tears. It was in these
days, that the minds of the Huckses unconsciously reverted to old times. It became
their wont, in these latter days, to sit in the
silent house, whence the children had gone
out to try issue with the world, and, of
evenings, to talk of the old faces and of the
old places, in the home of their youth.

Theirs had been a pinched and busy life. They had never returned to visit their old Ohio home. The Colonel's father and mother were gone. His wife's relatives were not there. Yet each felt the longing to go back. For years they had talked of the charms of the home of their childhood. Their children had been brought up to believe that the place was little less than heaven. The Kansas grass seemed short, and barren of beauty to them, beside the picture of the luxury of Ohio's fields. For them the Kansas streams did not ripple and dimple so merrily in the sun as the Ohio brooks, that romped through dewy pastures, in their memories. The bleak Kansas plain, in winter and in fall, seemed to the Colonel and his wife to be ugly and gaunt, when they remembered the brow of the hill under which their first kiss was shaded from the moon, while the world grew dim under a sleigh that bounded over the turnpike. The old people did not give voice to their musings. But in the woman's heart there gnawed a yearning for the beauty of the old scenes. It was almost a physical hunger.

After their last child, a girl, had married, and had gone down the lane toward the lights of the village, Mrs. Hucks began to watch with a greedy eye the dollars mount toward a substantial bank-account. She hoped that she and her husband might afford a holiday.

Last year, Providence blessed the Huckses with plenty. It was the woman, who revived the friendship of youth in her husband's cousin, who lives in the old township in Ohio. It was Mrs. Hucks, who secured from that cousin an invitation to spend a few weeks in the Ohio homestead. It was Mrs. Hucks, again, who made her husband happy by putting him into a tailor's suit — the first he had bought since his wedding — for the great occasion. Colonel Hucks needed no persuasion to take the trip. Indeed, it was his wife's economy which had kept him from being a spendthrift, and from borrowing money with which to go, on a dozen different occasions.

The day which Colonel and Mrs. William Hucks set apart for starting upon their journey was one of those perfect Kansas days in early October. The rain had washed the summer's dust from the air, clearing it, and stenciling the lights and shades very sharply. The woods along the little stream, which flowed through the farm, had not been greener at any time during the season. The second crop of grass on the hillside almost sheened in vividness. The yellow of the stubble in the grain fields was all but a glittering golden. The sky was a deep, glorious blue, and the big, downy clouds which lumbered lazily here and there in the depths of it, appeared near and palpable.

As Mrs. Hucks "did up" the breakfast dishes for the last time before leaving for the town to take the cars, she began to feel that the old house would be lonesome without her. The silence that was about to come, seemed to her to be seeping in, and it made her feel creepy. In her fancy she petted the furniture as she "set it to rights," saying mentally, that it would be a long time before the house would have her care again. To Mrs. Hucks every bit of furniture brought up its separate recollection, and there was a hatchet-scarred chair in the kitchen which had come with her in the wagon from Ohio. Mrs. Hucks felt that she could not leave that chair. All the while she was singing softly, as she went about her simple tasks. Her husband was puttering around the barnyard, with the dog under his feet. He was repeating for the twentieth time, the instructions to a neighbor about the care of the stock, when it occurred to him to go into the house and dress. After this was accomplished, the old couple paused outside the front door while Colonel Hucks fumbled with the key. "Think of it, Father," said Mrs. Hucks as she turned to descend from the porch. "Thirty years ago — and you and I have been fighting so hard out here — since you let me out of your arms to look after the horses. Think of what has come — and — and — gone, Father, and here we are alone, after it all."

"Now, Mother, I — " but the woman broke in again with:

"Do you mind how I looked that day? O, William, you were so fine, and so handsome then! What's become of my boy — my young—sweet—strong—glorious boy?"

Mrs. Hucks's eyes were wet, and her voice broke at the end of the sentence.

"Mother," said the Colonel, as he went around the corner of the house, "just wait a minute till I see if this kitchen door is fastened."

When he came back, he screwed up the corner of his mouth into a droll, one-sided smile and said, with a twinkle in his eyes, to the woman emerging from her handkerchief:

"Mother, for a woman of your age, I should say you had a mighty close call to being kissed, just then. That kitchen door was all that saved you."

"Now, Pa, don't be silly," was all that Mrs. Hucks had the courage to attempt, as she climbed into the buggy.

Colonel Hucks and his wife went down the road, each loath to go and leave the home-

place without their care. Their ragged, un-
even flow of talk was filled with more anxiety about the place which they were leaving, than it was with the joys anticipated
at their journey's end. The glories of Ohio,
and the wonderful green of its hills, and the
cool of its meadows, veined with purling
brooks, was a picture that seemed to fade in
the mental vision of this old pair, when they
turned the corner that hid their Kansas
home from view. Mrs. Hucks kept revert-
ing in her mind to her recollection of the
bedroom, which she had left in disorder. The
parlor and the kitchen formed a mental picture in the housewife's fancy, which did not
leave place for speculations about the glories
into which she was about to come. In the
cars, Colonel Hucks found himself leaning
across the aisle, bragging mildly about Kansas, for the benefit of a traveling man from
Cincinnati. When the Colonel and his wife
spread their supper on their knees in the
Kansas City Union Depot, the recollection
that it was the little buff Cochin pullet which
they were eating made Mrs. Hucks very

homesick.   The Colonel, on being reminded
of this, was meditative also.

They arrived at their destination in the
night.   Mrs. Hucks and the women of the
homestead refreshed old acquaintance in
the bedroom and in the kitchen, while the
Colonel and the men sat stiffly in the parlor,
and called the roll of the dead and absent.
In the morning, while he was waiting for his
breakfast, Colonel Hucks went for a prowl
down in the cow lot.   It seemed to him
that the creek which ran through the lot
was dry and ugly.   He found a stone upon
which as a boy he had stood and fished.
He remembered it as a huge boulder, and he
had told his children wonderful tales about
its great size.   It seemed to him that it had
worn away one half in thirty years.   The
moss on the river bank was faded and old,
and the beauty for which he had looked, was
marred by a thousand irregularities, which
he did not recall in the picture of the place
that he had carried in his memory since he
left it.

Colonel Hucks trudged up the bank from

the stream with his hands clasped behind
him, whistling "O, Lord, Remember me,"
and trying to reconcile the things he had
seen, with those he had expected to find.
At breakfast he said nothing of his puzzle,
but as Mrs. Hucks and the Colonel sat in
the parlor alone, during the morning, while
their cousins were arranging to take the
Kansas people over the neighborhood in the
buggy, Mrs. Hucks said:

"Father, I 've been lookin' out the window, and I see they 've had such a dreadful
drouth here. See that grass there, it 's as
short and dry—and the ground looks burn-
eder and crackeder than it does in Kansas."

"Uhm, yes," replied the Colonel. "I
had noticed that myself. Yet crops seem a
pretty fair yield this year."

As the buggy in which the two families
were riding rumbled over the bridge, the
Colonel, who was sitting in the front seat,
turned to the woman in the back seat and
said:

"Lookie there Mother, they 've got a
new mill — smaller'n the old mill, too."

To which his cousin responded, "Bill Hucks, what's got into you, anyway! That's the same old mill, where me and you used to steal pigeons."

The Colonel looked closer, and drawled out, "Well, I be doggoned! What makes it look so small? Ain't it smaller, Mother?" he asked, as they crossed the mill-race, that seemed to the Colonel to be a diminutive affair, compared with the roaring mill-race in which as a boy he had caught minnows.

The party rode on thus for half an hour, chatting leisurely, when Mrs. Hucks, who had been keenly watching the scenery for five minutes, pinched her husband and cried enthusiastically, as the buggy was descending a little knoll:

"Here 't is, Father! This is the place!"

"What place?" asked the Colonel, who was head over heels in the tariff.

"Do n't you know, William?" replied his wife with a tremble in her voice, which the woman beside her noticed.

Every one in the buggy was listening.

The Colonel looked about him; then, turning to the woman beside his wife on the back seat, he said:

"This is the place where I mighty nigh got tipped over trying to drive two horses to a sleigh, with the lines between my knees. Mother and me have remembered it, someway, ever since." And the old man stroked his grizzled beard, and tried to smile on the wrong side of his face, that the women might see his joke. They exchanged meaning glances when the Colonel turned away, and Mrs. Hucks was proudly happy. Even the dullness of the color on the grass, which she had remembered as a luscious green, did not sadden her for half an hour.

When the two Kansas people were alone that night, the Colonel asked:

"Do n't it seem kind of dwarfed here—to what you expected it would be? Seems to me like it 's all shriveled, and worn out, and old. Everything 's got dust on it. The grass by the roads is dusty. The trees that used to seem so tall and black with shade are just nothing like what they used to be.

The hills I 've thought of as young mountains do n't seem to be so big as our bluff
back — back home.''

Kansas was ''home'' to them now. For
thirty years the struggling couple on the
prairie had kept the phrase ''back home''
sacred to Ohio. Each felt a thrill at the
household blasphemy, and both were glad
that the Colonel had said ''back home,'' and
that it meant Kansas.

''Are you sorry you come, Father?'' said
Mrs. Hucks, as the Colonel was about to
fall into a doze.

''I do n't know, are you?'' he asked.

''Well, yes, I guess I am. I have n't no
heart for this, the way it is, and I 've some
way lost the picture I had fixed in my mind
of the way it was. I do n't care for this,
and yet it seems like I do, too. Oh, I wish
I had n't come, to find everything so washed
out — like it is!''

And so they looked at pictures of youth
through the eyes of age. How the colors
were faded! What a tragic difference there
is between the light which springs from the

dawn, and the glow which falls from the sunset.

After that first day Colonel Hucks did not restrain his bragging about Kansas. And Mrs. Hucks gave rein to her pride when she heard him. Before that day she had reserved a secret contempt for a Kansas boaster, and had ever wished that he might see what Ohio could do in the particular line which he was praising. But now, Mrs. Hucks caught herself saying to her hostess, ''What small ears of corn you raise here!''

The day after this concession Mrs. Hucks began to grow homesick. At first, she worried about the stock; the Colonel's chief care was about the dog. The fifth day's visit was their last. As they were driving to the town to take the train for Kansas, Mrs. Hucks overheard her husband discoursing, something after this fashion:

''I tell you, Jim, before I 'd slave my life out on an 'eighty' the way you 're doin', I 'd go out takin' in whitewashin'. It 's just like this — a man in Kansas has lower taxes, better schools, and more advantages in every way, than you 've got here. And as for grasshoppers? Why, Jim West, sech talk makes me tired! My boy Bill 's been always born and raised in Kansas, and now he 's in the legislature, and in all his life, since he can remember, he never seen a hopper. Would n't know one from a sacred ibex, if he met it in the road.''

While the women were sitting in the buggy at the depot waiting for the train, Mrs. Hucks found herself saying:

''And as for fruit — why, we fed apples to the hogs this fall. I sold the cherries, all but what was on one tree near the house, and I put up sixteen quarts from just two sides of that tree, and never stepped my foot off the ground to pick 'em.''

When they were comfortably seated on the homeward-bound train, Mrs. Hucks said to her husband:

''How do you suppose they live here in this country, anyway, Father? Do n't any one here seem to own any of the land joinin' them, and they 'd no more think of puttin'

in water tanks and windmills around their
farms than they 'd think of flyin'. I just
wish Mary could come out and see my new
kitchen sink with the hot and cold water in
it. Why, she almost fainted when I told
her how to fix a dreen for her dishwater
and things." Then after a sigh she added,
"But they are so onprogressive here, now-
a-days."

That was the music which the Colonel
loved, and he took up the strain, and carried the tune for a few miles. Then it became a duet, and the two old souls were
very happy.

They were overjoyed at being bound for
Kansas. They hungered for kindred spirits.
At Peoria, in the early morning, they
awakened from their chair-car naps to hear
a strident female voice saying:

"Well, sir, when the rain did finally come,
Mr. Morris he just did n't think there was
a thing left worth cutting on the place, but
lo, and behold, we got over forty bushel to
the acre off of that field, as it was."

The Colonel was thoroughly awake in an

instant, and he nudged his wife, as the voice went on:

"Mr. Morris he was so afraid the wheat was winter killed; all the papers said it was; and then come the late frost, which every one said had ruined it — but law me — "

Mrs. Hucks could stand it no longer. With her husband's cane she reached the owner of the voice, and said:

"Excuse me, ma'am, but what part of Kansas are you from?"

It seemed like a meeting with a dear relative. The rest of the journey to Kansas City was a hallelujah chorus, wherein the Colonel sang a powerful and telling bass.

When he crossed the Kansas state line Colonel Hucks began, indeed, to glory in his state. He pointed out the school-houses, that rose in every village, and he asked his fellow-passenger to note that the school-house is the most important piece of architecture in every group of buildings. He told the history of every rod of ground along the Kaw to Topeka. He dilated eloquently, and at length, upon the coal mines in Osage county, and he pointed with pride to the varied resources of his state. Every prospect was pleasing to Colonel Hucks, as he rode home that beautiful October day, and his wife was more radiantly happy than she had been for many years.

As the train pulled into the little town of Willow Creek, that afternoon, the Colonel craned his neck at the car window to catch the first glimpse of the big, red standpipe, and of the big stone school-house on the hill. When the whistle blew for the station, the Colonel said:

"What is it that fool Riley feller says about 'Grigsby's Station, where we used to be so happy and so pore'?"

As the Colonel and his wife passed out of the town into the quiet country, where the shadows were growing long and black, and where the gentle blue haze was hanging over the distant hills, that undulated the horizon, a silence fell upon the two hearts. Each mind sped back over a lifetime to the evening when they had turned out of the main road, in which they were traveling. A dog barking in the meadow behind the hedge did not startle them from their reveries. The restless cattle, wandering down the hillside toward the bars, made a natural complement to the picture which they loved.

"It is almost sunset, Father," said the wife, as she put her hand upon her husband's arm.

Her touch, and the voice in which she had spoken tightened some cord at his throat. The Colonel could only repeat, as he avoided her gaze:

"Yes, almost sunset, Mother, almost sunset."

"It has been a long day, William, but you have been good to me. Has it been a happy day for you, Father?"

The Colonel turned his head away. He was afraid to trust himself to speech. He clucked to the horses and drove down the lane. As they came into the yard, the Colonel put an arm about his wife and pressed his cheek against her face. Then he said drolly:

"Now, lookie at that dog,— come tearin' up here like he never saw white folks before!"

And so Colonel William Hucks brought his wife back to Kansas. Here their youth is woven into the very soil they love; here every tree around their home has its sacred history; here every sky above them recalls some day of trial and of hope.

Here in the gloaming to-night stands an old man, bent and grizzled. His eyes are dimmed with tears, which he would not acknowledge for the world, and he is dreaming strange dreams, while he listens to a little, cracked voice in the kitchen, half humming and half singing:

> " Home again, home again,
> From a foreign shore."

The Regeneration of Colonel Hucks

WHEN Colonel William Hucks, of Upper Slate Creek, in Center Township, better known as "Uncle Billy Hucks of Center," was elected delegate to the State Republican League convention at Topeka, in 1891, he untangled his legs from the low school-house desk where he had been sitting, and, rising, said that he supposed the members of the club knew what they were doing. He further said that he did n't need to tell them that he had been an Alliance man the year before, and had made a speech or two on the "Muddy" for the Alliance ticket, "though," he added with one of his smiles from the corner of his mouth, looking all over the room to assure the fellows that he was about to make a point, "I won't make any this

year." (Enthusiastic stamping of feet.)
"Not if I know myself." (More pedal enthusiasm.) But, nevertheless, the old man,
as he rode home that night, was a little
exercised over the prospect of being called a
traitor by his Alliance friends, and he wondered, rather unconsciously, if his declaration would n't look rather queer.

But when he thought of seeing all the old-
time Republican politicians at the "Copeland," and of shaking hands with "old
Plumb," and of hearing the speeches and
the resolutions, he forgot his doubts, hit
Bolivar an unusually hard lick as he came
down off the slant from the Slate Creek
bridge, and thereby showed that his spirits
were improving, and that his Rubicon had
been forded.

"Mother," said Colonel Hucks the next
morning, "I guess I will go to Topeky next
week."

"Is that so?" said Mrs. Hucks, who had
long since learned that the best way to find
out a thing was not to ask about it.

"Yes," said the Colonel. "There is

goin' to be some sort of a Republican doin's there, and I guess I better go."

And "Mother," whose father had "fit with old Grant," and whose brother had died at Shiloh, and whose faith in the war party had known no wavering, though her voice had been quiet for a year or so, only smiled and said, "I am glad to hear you are going, William, for you do need the rest."

But the Colonel knew what she meant.

The next week when he drove out of the front gate he was whistling "John Brown's Body." As he stopped to latch the gate, he could hear a thin, quavering, little voice, down at the spring house, as he had heard it before at the bean dinners, and the camp fires, and the rallies for a quarter of a century, singing with his own, "His soul goes marching on." Colonel Hucks recalled how proudly that little voice had sung that song at the ratification of his own election to the legislature, in the Center Township school-house, way back in the seventies. He remembered how she had taught the children at the township Sunday school to sing the song, before they could afford singing books.

On the main road an Alliance neighbor, afoot, climbed into the Colonel's wagon. The Colonel did not talk much, for his memory was wandering back to the time when little Link had died and they had buried him in the cute, blue soldier clothes "Mother" had made for the boy to play soldier in at the school exhibition; and the old man seemed to hear the children of the neighbors, as they gathered around the little, rough coffin, singing that song, the only song that every one knew:

"But his soul goes marching on."

"Got a pretty big cold, ain't you, Bill? It do n't pay to go to Republican meetings; the Lord is on our side," said the Alliance neighbor, who was riding beside him, and who had noticed the Colonel's watery eyes.

"You just go to hell a spell, will you?" growled the old man, as he sniffed and reached for a handkerchief.

But, for all this, the old doubt often had

been troubling him in his calmer moments.
Once, it came very strong, when the fellows
at the Center Township Alliance said he
would make a good county treasurer on the
Alliance ticket. When they started to pass
resolutions to that effect and to elect him
to the county convention, it was all Colonel
William Hucks could do to get up and tell
them that he was going up to Topeka on
some private and important business on the
day of the county convention. For he was
human. And being human, he was weak.
So when the county Alliance lecturer asked
him if he was really going as a delegate to
the Republican convention in Topeka, the
Colonel told the lecturer that he expected
to be in Topeka, anyhow, and that he supposed he would maybe drop in during the
afternoon and see what kind of a show the
Republicans could make when they tried.

The Colonel spread his name on the
" Copeland " register, " William Hucks,
Hucksville,'' and as the clerk was asking him,
"Will you have a room, Colonel Hucks?"
he saw the names of the heroes of his party,

the men who had made its speeches and written its platforms for a score of years — on the big register before his own; then it was that the old Doubt folded its tent. When he walked over to the convention hall and climbed the capitol steps with his wonted vigor, he stopped to look back and down to see if any of the "old fellows" were coming. He went into the governor's room, and found Lew Hanback there with a lot of "statesmen" around him. He stopped a moment to shake hands and then went on up stairs.

In the convention, the delegates were just getting down to business, and Burton was making a speech. The cheering had only begun, and he joined it. All the pent-up enthusiasm of the day, all the two years of compromised silence, during which he had been in training with the Alliance, found vent in that first yell he gave. He did n't really know what the speaker had said. He did n't care. He felt the "power." He wanted to cheer. And he cheered. He was n't afraid of anybody. He saw an Alli-

ance female lecturer in the gallery, and the
first time he caught her eye he put his hat
on the crook of his cane, and yelled like a
Fiji, when the speaker alluded to Blaine.
The others in the convention were not so
enthusiastic as he.   He thought them very
tame.   They were younger than Colonel
Hucks, and more careful of the proprieties.
But the Colonel was wedded to his idols,
and he did n't care whether school kept or
not.   He found he was put on the committee on resolutions, and he made a gallant
fight to have Blaine's name mentioned in
the committee's report.   But the young
man with the type-written set of resolutions
out-voted the Colonel; so in the convention
when the clause about reciprocity was read,
he led the delegates off with an old-fashioned "rouser."   The Colonel attracted so
much attention that the young fellows, who
were at the head of things, put his name up
as a candidate for some office or other, that
was being voted upon, but as he saw he
could n't make it, he withdrew.   While on
his feet, he was tempted to make a school-

house speech, but he lacked courage, and sat down.

The Colonel's soul was at peace, and he was happy.

But when the "Capital" reporter came to him for an interview, after adjournment, the Colonel's cup ran over. Before this, there had always been so many big fellows at the state conventions, that Colonel Hucks had not been worth an interview, from a newspaper standpoint.

He had once achieved the proud distinction of having his name mis-spelled in the personal column of the "Capital," in connection with being a guest at the "Copeland," and of reporting "crops in fine condition in the Slate Valley"; but he had never before been interviewed by a real city reporter. He wondered what they would say, when they read this at home. He would have stayed with that reporter all day, if he had not heard some one behind him say, "Plumb 's come, Plumb 's come!"

This talismanic signal passed around the lobby of the hotel, with telegraphic rapidity.

And the Colonel joined the procession, which was headed toward the Senator.

Plumb was a little heavier and a little paler than he had been on the day when Colonel Hucks voted for him for Senator in the legislature, but otherwise he was unchanged. The great man leaned forward with his head on one side, and extended to the Colonel one hand, putting the other upon the farmer's shoulder. "I hear you have been helping the Alliance and the rebels pass the force bill, Colonel," said the Senator, smiling. "Your pension comes all right now, do n't it? Did you get that horse book you sent for? I spoke to Rusk about it, and he said he 'd answer you. Why, hello there, Jim, how are you?" And before he knew it, the Colonel found himself explaining to the crowd how he had written to Plumb for one of Jerry Rusk's "agricultural reports," and how he 'd got a letter from Rusk saying that they were all out, but that m'm'm', and the hum of the other voices drowned his own.

At night, when Plumb was on the rostrum, Colonel Hucks was tired. The old man's applause, instead of being what the papers call "loud and continuous," was of the kind which nods the head, and nudges the man sitting next, and claps the hands. He followed the Senator pretty closely, and when the speaker alluded to those "on whose heads have fallen the snow which never melts," the Colonel caught his eye, and the pathos of the remark brought the moisture to his own. After that, the old man nearly nodded his head off with approbation. When "Joe" Ady roasted the Alliance, the Colonel felt rested, and his loyal whoop led the applause; its echo was the last to die after the speech had closed.

When he got back to Willow Creek, his county seat, the next day, the Colonel went to the office of the Lincoln County "Republican," wherein that week appeared this item:

"Colonel William Hucks, of Hucksville, the war-horse of Center Township, was in town last night on his return from the State

Republican League convention, and made this office a pleasant call. Colonel Hucks has been in training with the Alliance for the past eighteen months, but he authorizes us to say that he is back in the fold and hopes the ninety and nine will rejoice with him. Uncle Billy raised the biggest crop of wheat ever raised on Slate Creek, and all of the corn in his 200 acre field was sold by him this morning for $15 an acre. He left the wherewithal to pay for one year's subscription to this great family newspaper and the State "Capital" for one year. Uncle Billy, you 're a daisy, and here's our ☞"

As he drove into his front yard that night he noticed the old regimental flag waving over the door. Inside of the house, he observed that "Mother" had brought out the pictures of Grant and Sherman and Lincoln, which she had put away the year before. They were hanging in the best room with little "Link's" faded blue soldier-cap in the center of the group.

"Did you have a nice time at Topeky, William?"

"Yes, Mother," and after a pause he

added, as he looked at the little cap and the old flag, which now and then floated in through the door, "and say, Mother, 'his soul goes marching on.'"

For Colonel William Hucks was never what you would call a "soft" man.

The Undertaker's Trust

THERE was Riggs's bill for hay; that was $7. There was Morse's bill for pasture, due the day before, that was $3.75, and there was the old bill against Judge Blair for butter and milk, $6.70, and nothing had been paid on it for two months. It really seemed to Captain Meyers, picking his way along the rough stone walk upon the side streets and often walking in the path beside it, that there would be no difficulty at all in collecting the $5, that he and his wife had decided to spend upon their daughter Mattie's birthday present. The Captain made up his mind, as he trudged along, to collect all the money, and to buy the present that afternoon and have it over with. And to that end, he hurried past Riggs's livery barn, and on toward the postoffice, acting on the theory that if he went to the barn so soon after dinner, he would not find Riggs there. It was just mail time, when the Captain arrived at the postoffice. He waited there patiently, while the mail was distributed, and looked at the trinkets in the jeweler's case in the front part of the lobby. He fancied a certain gold and onyx pin, which he had looked at in the morning, and which he had then decided to buy for his daughter's birthday present, with the money he was about to collect. He knew that his wife wanted the family present to be a new dress; there had been some discussion on the subject before he left the house that noon, after the child had gone to school, but the Captain's heart was set on the pin. And as he stood peering into the glass case, his faith in it became firmly fixed. He might have bought the pin then and there, but he feared he would be refused credit, and the prospect of a humiliating refusal frequently kept the Captain out of debt. As he was feasting his eyes upon the pin, his neighbor, John Morse, who owed the Captain for pasture rent, elbowed along beside him.

"Hullo, John," said the Captain, looking up suddenly and recollecting that he was going to collect his bill during the afternoon, and a little fluttered at the prospect. "They make a lot of durn fool purties — them jewelers — do n't they? Keep a feller pore just to look at 'em purt' nigh, do n't you think?"

"I dunno, Cap," replied the other man, who was a trifle ill at ease in the presence of his creditor, and wished to ward off a dunning. "I dunno; I s'pose its as easy to get pore lookin' at the fixin's, as it is a-layin' 'round doin' nothin', as a feller's got to do, these days. And when you do get a little job of work it seems like you can't never get the money on it."

Here Captain Meyers's heart sank; he was being outgeneraled, and he knew it. Morse went on: "I done a little job over here for Major Hanley the other day, and went down this mornin' to collect it — thought mebbe might get a little somethin' and square up with you and a few odd bills around — but, by Johnny, if Major did n't stand me off till the first of the month."

The crowd was moving, and the Captain knew that the delivery window of the post-office was open. He did n't want to seem a hard man with his neighbors, so he said, as they walked toward the center of the crowd: "Oh, well, John, me and you understand each other; you need n't to go and worry about that little business of mine; I ain't in no rush."

The Captain's "Veteran's Defender" was in his box, and when he had put it in his pocket, he drifted in the current of the crowd, and found himself being carried up the broad smooth stone sidewalks of the business street to the row of straggling, one-story frame offices, carpenter shops, and millinery stores, that marked the dividing line between the residence and business portions of the town. As he came to the crossing, a buggy bumping over the stones stopped the group of which he was a member.

"Who's that with Riggs in the buggy?" asked the Captain.

"Oh, him? Why that's a drummer; I heard him say he was going to drive over to Fairview to catch the main-line South, to-night," said an elderly member of the party, who responded when any one spoke to the "colonel." It would be wrong to say that Captain Meyers's heart sank at hearing this, for he thought with a feeling of relief that to-morrow would be the best time to collect Riggs's bill, anyway. The group sauntered into one of the little offices, as was the custom of its members, and the Captain told himself that he would wait until Judge Blair had finished his mail before disturbing him.

The Colonel, and "Doc," and "J. L.," and the Captain, that was the coterie. They had become cronies during the years that followed the "boom" and left them idle. The Colonel had been county surveyor, "Doc" had been coroner years ago, before the young doctors crowded him out of his practice, and "J. L." was the real estate dealer, who owned the office. Captain Meyers had been county clerk two terms, deputy one term,

then city clerk, and finally, constable; he
was sometimes made deputy sheriff when
there was extra work.   But he was at the
end of his political rope. By close living his
wife had saved the farm near town, which
was their homestead, before they moved to
the county seat. She had saved a little
money, which was at interest, and the
family lived off the farm and small sums
coming from chickens, and butter, and eggs.
The Captain's only child was the girl — Mattie — thirteen years old, and on her he lav-
ished the affection of a heart still mellow.
As he sat in the office "gassing" with the
crowd, he thought of the pin and how beautiful it was, and how the child would enjoy
it, and he almost lost the thread of the conversation.

"Do n't you, Cap?" said the Colonel.

"Do n't I what? ' said the Captain, wak-
ing from his reverie, "I do, if you say I do,
but what is it?"

"Well," explained the first speaker, "I
was just sayin' that there was just as smart
folks down here on the 'Crick' as they is

up there in the city, if they only had the
swing that the other fellows had.   And I
said that 's what you said, do n't you,
Cap'n?''

"That 's just what I've contended all the
time; do n't take no smarter man to run a
railroad than to run a street car line; and
do n't take no more brains to run a street
car 'n it does to run a stage line, and no
more to run a stage 'n it does to run a dray,
and a man that can't run a dray ain't
worth his salt.''

"That 's right,'' broke in the real estate
man. "I 've seen it worked time and again.
Now take that Rushmer feller; warn't so
overly much down here; I done him up,
myself, in a little deal in College Hill lots.
Now look at him; up there in the city, got
a carriage and nigger driver, and every one
thinks he 's old persimmons. It 's all owin'
to the length of the leever you 're a workin'
with.   If you 're workin' with cents, you
make cents; if the handle of your leever is
a little longer and you 're workin' with dollars, you, make dollars; if it 's hundreds,

you make hundreds; and if it 's thousands
you get your picture in the paper as a
'Napoleon of finance.' ''

"I guess that 's mighty near the truth,"
said the Doctor in the sententious pause
that followed.

The Captain was just starting for Judge
Blair's to collect the butter and milk bill,
when he saw the Judge come out of his
office and go down street.   He settled back
in his seat by the window, to wait until the
Judge returned.   The talk droned along.
From ''Napoleons of finance'' it turned to
trusts, and from trusts to the great fortunes
made in the insurance business.   And it
must have been nearly four o'clock when
the Captain held the reins of the rambling
discourse, and was guiding it by mere impulse as follows:

"Yes, sir; a undertaker's insurance company.   A sort of undertaker's trust.   F'r in-
stance, say our man Nichols here belonged;
s'pose I 'd pay him say $5 a year, and
would agree to keep it up for the rest of my
life, if he would give me a certain specified

burial. All right; say I move away from here. Very well; I have my receipt — my policy — from old man Nichols — and I go to the town where I move to, and take it to the member of the insurance company, or trust, or what you may call it, that lives there, and pay him while I live there; then if I move on I keep transferrin' my policy, and at last I'm buried in style, and my family ain't out a red. The trust has got the money, and if I only pay the last man a $5 bill, the trust pays him for givin' me a good burial. They have the use of my money; I do n't feel it; all right — and in the end it ain't hard for my family to raise the money, when they do n't know where to turn to get it. Rates can be just like insurance rates, high or low, accordin' to the age a man is and the style he wants to go out with.''

"Then your idee," put in the real estate man, "is to take dyin' out of the luxuries of the rich and put it in the reach of all.''

The crowd laughed.

Captain Meyers laughed with the rest,

but his eyes glowed, and he was filled with
the scheme that had evolved from his talk.
It seemed so plain and feasible to him — this
plan of forming an undertaker's trust to in-
sure men decent burial.   He saw that if he
could get a place at the head of such an en-
terprise, and push it to a reality, he would
be rich. He was afraid lest some of his companions should see the value of the idea,
and he let the talk roll over him, saying
nothing further of what was in his mind.

Judge Blair, passing along the street toward his office, aroused the Captain from
his castle building. As he crossed the street
to Judge Blair's office, he concluded to take
the Judge into his plans.   He would need
a partner, and a lawyer and a man of the
world, he thought.   Judge Blair was three
in one and one in three — the very trinity
he wanted. The Judge was the county
politician; he knew all the statesmen in the
state; he knew the bankers and the lawyers
and the editors in the big city. In fact, when
any one spoke of Willow Creek, beyond its
corporate limits, he always spoke of it as

Judge Blair's town. Judge Blair was always in debt, yet his credit remained good, because he paid in smiles and patronage and railroad passes, what he could not pay in cash; so the town took what he had to offer, and discounted it by pitying him for what it called "his extravagant family." He was Captain Meyers's idol; he sometimes paid the Captain money — an unusual distinction — and he always got the Captain railroad passes to the state G. A. R. reunions. The Captain was fairly bubbling with enthusiasm, when he reached Judge Blair's private office. The Judge thought Captain Meyers had come to ask for money, as in fact he had; he really intended to get it before he left, but he poured out his plans first, almost in a breath. "What do you think of it, Judge?" he asked, after the first pause, when the Judge had just finished telling him that it looked feasible. "Don't you think it will go? Everybody's got to die, and everyone wants a nice funeral. What do they join lodges for, if they don't? We get the use of the man's money; we get the profits on funeral expenses before they are incurred. We could issue ten, twenty, and twenty-five year policies, and with a certificate on him a man could move anywhere, and be sure of a good funeral. Say, Judge, won't you take holt of this? It 's a big thing, Judge, a mighty big thing. What say, Judge, is it a go?'' They talked until the gloaming fell, and walked home in the sunset glow, stopping for half an hour at the parting of their ways to go over again the elaborated scheme.

Captain Meyers, who always came in through the back door of his house, brought a load of wood in his arms, this evening, as a flag of truce. He wanted to make peace with his wife before she asked about the afternoon's collections. Mattie was "laying" the supper table as he entered the kitchen door, and his wife was busy over the stove. He spoke as he laid down the wood. "Ma, I 've had a good talk with Judge Blair this afternoon; him and me stopped down there at Nichols's corner a few minutes and that 's what made me late.''

There was something in his voice which the woman recognized to distrust. She saw he was manœuvering; it angered her; she knew he had not collected the bills she had given him; she knew very well he was trying to talk her out of scolding him. She was a large woman, fat and lusty. He was much older, and thinner, and less vigorous than she. She was cruel to him that night, as she often was, and his great scheme only unfolded itself as an apology for his idleness, after she had rebuked him; it did not come as he would have had it come, as a justification for forgetting everything else. His daughter did not understand it at all, but when he had finished, and stood leaning on the threshold of the dining-room door, hesitating, she beckoned him into the room where she was clattering the knives and forks. She gave him a good girlish hug and a kiss, and pointed to a plate of corn bread near his plate. He knew that she had made it for him. Her mother did not eat it, and never cooked it, though it was his favorite dish.

"Now, Mattie, what'd you go and cook that for," he said, "and get yourself all played out for the party? I could 'a' ate light bread just as well."

But he patted her cheek as he said it, and sat on the lounge and watched her lovingly, as she went about her task. And he lay awake far into the night furnishing an air castle with ivory and gold, wherein his daughter was to be the queen.

The next day was Mattie's birthday; Judge Blair had gone out of town. The Captain felt that it would do no good to see his neighbor Morse, after the rebuff of the previous day. He was afraid to delay a minute in seeing Riggs, and yet he feared to see him, for on him, alone, lay all his hopes; he knew that he must have that $7 hay bill, or forego the onyx pin, and his heart was set on that. He walked past Riggs's livery barn to the postoffice, the first thing in the morning, and looked at the pin in the jeweler's case, in walking by.

He faltered, as he eyed it, coming from the postoffice wicket; the jeweler saw him;

there was no one in the lobby that morning. "Can we show you anything this morning, Cap'n?" asked the clerk, turning from his work bench with a rubber-cased microscope stuck over his eye.

"Nothin' partic'lar — well, I do n't know, but what you can let me look at that onyx pin you was showin' me here the other day."

He carried the image of the pin in his mind to Riggs's stable; it made him bold to clear his throat before saying, "Well, Jim Riggs, how 'd you and that drummer make it yesterday, goin' over to Fairview?"

"M — hm — n, I dunno; all right, I guess," replied the liveryman, who knew what was coming.

"Well — say — Jim — would it be pushing you too much to ask you for a little something on the hay account?" It was out, and the Captain knew he had said it poorly. To mend it, he added, "I 'm needin' it, right now for a little matter."

Of course, he did n't get it, and when he met Mattie on the street, coming home,

from school, he sent word to her mother that
he was busy and would not be home to
dinner.   He forgot all about the undertaker's trust that day, as he walked listlessly
from one loafing place to another, and back
again, trying to get away from the dread of
going home empty-handed at nightfall.   He
lounged into the postoffice with the crowd
at mail time, in the afternoon, and gazed
longingly at the coveted jewel.   But he
could not bring himself to ask for credit,
especially since he had said in the morning
that he was coming around to get the pin
when he got some money, and the jeweler
had not taken the hint.   He felt of the half
dollar in his pocket, and looked at everything which he thought could be had for
that sum, but nothing suited his purpose.

It was nearly sundown, when a peddler of
whittled trinkets stumbled into the real
estate office where the cronies were loafing.
The peddler was an oldish man, and claimed
to be blind.   The fact that he had whittled
the intricate fancies, although he was blind,
lent value to them in the eyes of his cus-

tomers. There was a large, circular piece of pine, fretted with holes and with serrated edges; it was made from one block of wood.

"What's that wheel business for?" asked "J. L." of the vender.

"Oh, that? That's just a kind of a purty; a card case some uses 'em fer."

"What's it worth?" asked a curious bystander.

"I get a dollar and a half for them," responded the peddler, holding it up to show it to advantage.

The Captain was rolling his fifty-cent piece idly in his pocket, when the answer came. Suddenly desperation seized him at the thought of going home on his child's birthday without a present, and as the peddler was moving out of the door, Captain Meyer said:

"I'll give you fifty cents for that whirl-a-ma-gig, thing-a-ma-bob card case, or whatever you call it."

It was the last one the peddler had, and he took the Captain's money.

The child met her father at the gate, and took his arm as they walked down the path. The thought of the gold and onyx pin made the wooden trifle he carried in the hand farthest from her seem very cheap to him.

"It is n't much, Mattie," he said as they reached the front steps, "but I thought maybe you 'd understand it was all your ma and me could do. It 'll look purty on the organ, or on the center table. The man said it was a card case." The old man's voice faltered as he went on: "Maybe at your next birthday your pa will have more to do with."

He was thinking of the undertaker's trust. The child was her father's child, and she hugged him and thanked him over and over again for the toy. It made him happy, and he was radiant in her reflected smiles. They had gone around the house to the kitchen door when the girl said: "And oh, Pa, did you see the gold and onyx pin Ma brought me from the store this afternoon?"

Captain Meyers kissed his wife for the first time in years. It was all over so quickly that she did not think to scold, but mingled her tears with his, and her laughter with that of the child.

"That's For Remembrance."

IN the morning the house, which faced eastward, presented a square expanse of white stone shining in the sun through a bower of old elms. It sat somewhat further back in the lot than most houses on the street, and at night the shadows of the elm branches almost hid it.

When the night was windy,—and it is often windy in this zone,—the great square house came in and out of the shadows, as the branches bent to disclose it, and then to hide it, like a ghostly thing.

The house was a generation old, and in the corners and upon certain sides, ivy had grown. The ivy made it seem less austere; yet its straight lines at the eaves, its unbroken sides, its high porches unrelieved by fret-work or gewgaws, despite the softening ivy, gave it something of a sepulchral look.

The wayfarer thought, as he passed it, of great cheerless rooms, with high ceilings and damp walls.

On a night when the autumn leaves rode the gusty wind, a man and a woman alighted from a public carriage in front of the house, and proceeded to its doorway where the man unlocked the door and the two entered. It was not yet midnight. They were evidently expected, for the servants had lighted the fire in the grates, and an electric bulb glowed in the hallway.

Just inside the door the man and woman, finding there was no servant in sight or hearing, embraced rapturously, and walked, entwined in each other's arms, through a double door to a sparkling fire.

Their voices were low and sweet. They had been married a month; it was their home coming. The bluster of the wind outside made the fire feel grateful. They sat almost silently in sheer joy before it, for a few moments. The woman rose to go to another room. The man detained her. He said:

"Sweetheart, wait a minute, won't.you?"

She came to his side with a word of endearment and a caress that had even then become almost a habit.

"You won't mind, will you darling, if I talk just a little bit about Ruth — right now — will you?"

A look answered; he went on. "You know she was a very good woman" — he was going to say "little woman," but checked it. The wife only pressed her husband's arm. She was a woman of twenty-eight, and very sane.

"She always wanted me to — to do this, to marry again. The man stammered.

"I suppose so," said his wife.

"Yes" — the man continued — "and darling, one day just before the last — she made me promise one thing. It was all she ever asked, and I—I—, you would n't have me break it, would you?"

His wife pressed his arm reassuringly, and he went over to a desk and there in a drawer found a large manilla envelope addressed to "Mr. and Mrs. James Gordon." The writing was a woman's.　He crossed the room to his wife with the envelope.

She watched him curiously.　He was visibly embarrassed.　The woman advanced and said:

"What is it, James, do n't be afraid of me.　My poor boy, I honor you so much for this."

She had not seen the envelope.　When she saw it, she looked surprised.

"Yes," said the man — noting her look. "It 's her writing — Ruth's — I promised I'd open it the night I brought any one — you know — home.　She was a sick child, Margaret, and —"　He feared to go further in deprecation.　He knew he should despise himself if he did, and he feared his wife would despise him.

He tore open the envelope and two smaller white ones, each addressed — one to James Gordon, and the other to Mrs. James Gordon, fell out on the table.

"I think," said the husband, "she desired us to read them.　Can you for me — Margaret?" he asked.

The woman snapped on an electric current, and taking her letter from its sheath, read, while her husband did the same. They were sitting by the fire as they read. The man's epistle was the shorter. It was this:

"My Dear, Dear Boy: — I wanted so to be resurrected for a minute or two,— real and alive to you, and I thought it all over so many times at the last, Jim, and I said, I want to be with Jim when he is like he was when I know he was the happiest. I did n't want to come back for the last time to a sad, tearful Jim, but to just my Jim as he was when I loved him best. It will make me happier to see you as you are to-night, Jim. Oh! it makes me so happy to see you happy, my boy. I must not stay any longer; it will make you feel bad, and I won't be a selfish thing. Now that I 've seen you, my own Jim, and had this little talk with you, I do n't mind it at all. Oh! goodbye Jim, goodbye, goodbye! Oh! I — I — no I must not say that — just good-bye. RUTH." The other letter ran thus:

"My Dear Mrs. Gordon: You won't

be jealous of a poor dead woman, will you?
Nor grudge her just a minute out of your
joy.   I 'm so glad you married Jim, and
you know I wanted to see you and him
right now at your happiest.   Is n't life
good?   I won't ever come back any more,
and ·you won't blame me for being a little
childish to-night. I 'll tell you what, I did n't
feel it right to tell Jim — that I love him.
There, I 've said it, — and he was my God.
You must not tell him this nor anything,
but you 'll like Jim better, and me too, for
saying it.   It feels good to wash my soul of
all dross and give Jim to you — all of him.
But, O, my dear, my dear, be good to him.
He has a gentle heart, has my — your boy.
God bless him and you.   I was going to
sign Mrs. Ruth Gordon, but I can 't, can I?
Is n't it strange?   You 'll be good to Jim
now, won't you?   Yours,"

"RUTH MASON."

The woman walked to the grate and
burned her letter without saying a word.
The man, who was standing near her, let his
paper slip and fall into the flames.   Each sat

down, and the gust of wind clicked a latch
somewhere in the great house.   This startled them.   Each saw that there was a vacant chair between them.   Something
clutched sharply at each heart a moment,
then the woman crept swiftly to the man
with a sob, and life—warm and sweet with
love, took up its rushing course again.

A Nocturne.

NIGHT, and the stars, and the summer moon, large and opulent in yellow splendor, drifting on the billows that the soft south wind makes in the tops of the eastern elm trees; night, and the stars, and the quiet of the country, the large somber quiet, dotted here and there by the tinkle of country cow-bells, rumpled with the prattle of distant waters that the wind brings now and then; night, and the stars, and voices that blow from nowhere into dreams and are lost in the blur of intoxicated fancies which come trooping across the mind's well-beaten playground; night, and the stars, and love—the visions that young men see, and the dreams that old men cherish; night, and the stars, and the powerful spell of the half lights, the conjurer's draught working its great mystery upon the heart; here they sit under the night and the stars — comrades. They had been boys in the old days together. Perhaps to many reckoners of time the old days had not seemed far distant—a year, a decade — they are long at the threshold of youth, where small events are shaping eternal destinies. The old days to these two meant the dear days — the very young days, the days of guitar strings, and love songs, and oar-locks.

These comrades had come back to the little town, one from the East, one from the West, and were sitting on the hill where they had stood of old. They were watching the lights twinkle and fade in the village. The roll of the absent ones had been called, and re-called, and names that each wished left unspoken were consciously breathed in a dozen silences. They were not so old; yet the dead were there. They were not so young that life was new to them. The night was a joy to them because its reminiscences were fresh; its potation exhilarated them with real thrills of

hopes unexpressed — that delirium which
youth has stolen from the barbaric gods.
Faces, places, fancies passed them in bright
review, and, filled with the maudlin witch-
ery of the night and its brew, in a silence
that fell gently between the two, the
younger man lifted his voice in an old song
that had been an outlet for their efferves-
cent spirits in the other days.   In those
days they had roared it out, dwelling on
the garish cadences, bearing down on the
rude and imperfect sequences of harmony,
and welling forth their youthful exuberance
in a bubble of song.   Now they were glad
when the verse ended that they might clear
their throats as the song went on, and half
of the forgotten stanza came out, "dah,
dah."   The chorus ran:

> "How the old folks would enjoy it!
> They would sit all night and listen
> As we sang in the evening
> By the moonlight."

They crooned rather than sang the ballad;
there was no spring, no clink of youth to
the voices that sighed the old song.   The

words even now passed unheeded from their lips. He who took the tenor part could not reach the high notes, so he sang in unison with the other in places. It was not much past midnight, yet each felt his bed drawing him to it. After the song, they sat listening to the ripples of sound that beat upon the shore of the night.

Suddenly below them, from some recently unhoused evening gathering, came a song, whose melody throbbed to the chords of a guitar. "Bring back, bring back, bring back my bonnie to me," came the old song. The two comrades sat mute. It was such a lusty song; the notes were so full of animal vigor. The holds in the tune were clutched firmly by the virile tenors and voluptuous contraltos.

> "My Bonnie lies over the ocean,
> My Bonnie lies over the sea,
> My Bonnie lies over the ocean,
> Oh, bring back my Bonnie to me!"

"They sing well, do n't they?" said one of the comrades, while the guitar was hunting for the thread of some fresh melody.

'Yes; I could sit here all night and hear them sing.   It is as in a looking-glass.''

The voice that replied was drowned in the other's ears by a new burst of song.

"Nita, Juanita, ask thy soul if we must part," sang the glad voices—voices caressing and pledging other voices as the glowing harmony rose.

"Flitting, flitting away,
    All that we cherish most dear;
The violets pass with the May,
    The roses must die with the year."

What did they who sang know of the words they sang?   The two men on the hill were silent, and the stars gleamed through moist eyes.   There was a lull in the singing.   Neither man spoke for awhile, then a voice said:

"It was good, wasn't it?—like old times."

"Yes—old times.   I wish they would go on singing.   Are you tired?"

"No; I would never tire of that, would you?"   Then from somewhat further down the street came the song:

"In the evening by the moonlight,
 You could hear those banjoes ringing;
In the evening by the moonlight
 You could hear those voices singing.
How the old folks would enjoy it!
They would sit all night and listen
As we sang in the evening
 By the moonlight."

That was the last song. The comrades sat for a few moments longer with lumpy throats, and then, arm in arm, walked down the hill. At the parting of their ways, the song each had been humming in his mind tried to find their lips:

"How the old folks—"

It broke then in a nervous laugh, and a flash of interrogatory silence. Then — ·

"Yes, Jim — you see it, too."

And he who was addressed replied: "I knew you would understand."

"I suppose, Jim, we are old folks. It is our part now 'to sit all night and listen.' "

"To listen and dream, Joe — I think we never understood the words before."

And so they parted, there under the night and the stars, and each fumbled over and over in his heart that new phrase, "old folk"—while the tune gamboled lightly through a dozen hearts that night, and chased lovers' phantasies out into the star-dimpled field of dreams, out into the night, and the summer and the moon and the quiet of the country, large, and sweet, and wistful as an absent sweetheart's musings— herself gazing out at the moonlit night.

PRINTED AT THE LAKESIDE PRESS
BY R. R. DONNELLEY AND SONS CO
MDCCCXCVI